Autumn's Torch

Sje Mohntoh

Potion A

1

Aimlessly wandering about
day in and day out
another week goes by
a month or two
then another year dies

In the beginning
there is no spring
no showers
for blooming flowers
no song birds that sing

Summer's glory
never comes to my release
no morning rise
to set up evening tide
no moon to ease restless peace

From birth to dirt
between every footstep
that touches earth

my whole life suspends
in autumn

Falling leaves
a crisp bone chilling breeze
signifies the nature of
my demise
like a lingering death
smoldering right by
my side

Winter's crypt
has always been
a step or two away
a shadowy wave hovers over me
which destines my nights
and dooms my days

It matters not
if I'm in my youth
or in my age of old
impossible to resist
the imminence of my death
that fate holds

Lighter part of night, darker part of day is suspended. Twilight dawn holds its pause. A new day commences. Slowly, it rolls out of early to late morning into the center of time.

In a stupor mood, he sits at a wooden table and a chair pounding shots of the most potent liquor he can afford. Several paintings set on the floor against the wall of a room with barely any other furniture. The natural outside lighting comes through a window indicating a drab, cloudy mid-afternoon day. He glares up at the ceiling. A rope with a noose is tied firmly in place. One shot after another, he continues plastering his senses to becoming dull to emotions and feelings. After every two shots, he looks up to see what he has rigged, and then more of the same pounding of ocean roars of alcohol drowning his inner system. Once he thinks he has enough, he stops and leans back in his chair. Fear is no longer there. It is replaced with melancholy. There is no thinking. He acts on impulse.

He clears the table in one swoop with his arm, leaps onto the table, and wraps the noose around his neck, kicking the table away from his support. His weight and positioning gives a slight swing of his body as he hangs without a fight. The rope squeezes his neck blocking air passage to his brain and encloses blood to his head. His eyes begin to bulge. He suddenly realizes this is not the perfect way to go. Another way can be quicker and simpler. He struggles to release the rope from around his neck, making his body swing violently to and fro. He gasps for air. His voice is left speechless as he attempts to yell, shout, or scream. Kicking in midair, throwing his body into contortions, the ceiling plaster begins to crumble because of his body weight and the force of gravity. His fight against death begins to recede. His legs become still; his arms are pinned to the sides of his body; his head drops. Forty-five seconds later, the plastered ceiling gives way and releases the apparatus which supports the rope of death. He crashes to the floor. There is no motion for quite some time. Slowly, his eyes open. He notices the room illuminating a brighter light from outside because of a cloud has rolled a lighter shade of gray.

Barely enough strength, he gingerly unties the noose from around his neck. Someone bangs a fist on the outside of the door. A woman's voice of many years speaks.

"Hey in there! You better not be destroying anything! You still got last month's rent to pay!"

He quietly lies there until the beating on the door and shouts from her voice is no longer heard.

Time in life, in age, may be synonymous to seasons in nature. A man of 45 years by the name of Cidal, an African-American who has never been married nor has he ever fathered any children. An artist as he is, he has worked many odd jobs in order to support himself and to supplement sparsely income from his art. Living in a world of modern technology with internet speed and web design, it is very rare for one to indulge creative juices using a simple canvass, paint brushes, and colors, all by the stroke of a delicate hand. Patience and endurance are ingredients to success when results are not as quickly available by the click of a mouse or the tap of a computer key.

All of his life, most of his life, his current life is trying to find his way. Raised in an orphanage, Cidal walks the path of a loner. From past to present, he usually is by himself…stands and walks alone. This is of no concern to him. He is used to it. He has never known anything else. His life is his to which no one else can claim. It is his to keep or to take.

The landlady, Ms. Pearly, an African-American woman of 65 plus years, with bluish hair, wearing pointed rimmed glasses, presses her ear against the door. She is silent. Cidal remains quiet to collect his thoughts after the stroke of death, and to make certain she is gone. Neither one budges. Both are at a standstill. When he thinks she is gone, he gets up to brush the dust and debris from his clothes. Without any grace, he staggers over and plops on the floor where a shot glass and one-fourth liquor remains in the bottle. He turns up the bottle to down the rest of the content.

Cidal goes to the bathroom to refresh. Splashes cold water to his face and tidies up his appearance and then returns to the living room. He needs an idea to bring focus to his paintings. Walking in nature usually helps his spirit to create his artwork. He looks back at his creation leaning against the wall of the room. He turns to head out.

When he opens the door…

Ms. Pearly stands with folded arms. She tries to look around him to see inside of the apartment, but he blocks her view with his body and partially closed door.

"What have you been doing in there?" she demands.

"Nothing, ma'am. Just some artwork."

"Let me see."

"No, I can't. We're funny about people looking at our un-finished pieces."

"I believe there's some funny business going on in there."

"Not this time. Things are quite serious."

"You better be handing over some serious money. You're a month behind."

"I've always been good in paying up. You'll have it by the end of the week."

"Only reason why I'm so lenient with you is because you remind me of my nephew. Okay. By Friday, I want my money."

"Saturday at the latest. I'll shoot for Friday though."

No words, she heads downstairs from the second floor apartment home dwelling. To make sure his path is clear from spying, curious eyes, Cidal closes the door so Ms. Pearly can hear that he is back inside. Then he quietly opens the door and lurks out to find she is gone for good. His wait is for more than one minute but less than two. Then, he cleverly leaves without notice.

2

Living in the town of Rising Falls, Cidal can walk out of his apartment home and be surrounded by everything he needs. Unlike many American cities, Rising Falls has unique qualities similar to non-western countries. Restaurants, open-markets, street vendors, shopping mall, grocery stores, office buildings, hotels, movie theater, and other stores and shops that cater to every human need from personal care to items of want or leisure. Pedestrians walk; cyclists ride their motorbikes; drivers in automobiles; taxis; buses. The streets and sidewalks are kept pretty clean considering the amount of people to and fro. A large park in the center of town called the Garden Square where people gather for social events or relaxation. The mood in the entire atmosphere is laidback…unrushed.

Rising Falls was developed by former slaves back in late 1800's. The community expanded through early 20th century, developing businesses, commerce, and evolving creative art: Music, literature, performing acts, paintings, and sculptures. By middle to late century, and well into 21st century, other people of color with different ethnicities as in Latinos, Asians, Indians, and some Arabs increased in population, but never became the majority. The fairest skin tone is present but clearly in the minority range. There is peace amongst the inhabitants without conflict or a great divide that plague other cities in America. Law enforcement of color has good community relations with the citizens it serves by immersing within the circles of the population instead of distancing themselves on its periphery.

Cidal wants, needs fresh air after the attempt on his own life. He dares not take his motorbike because of the influence of the high potent liquid that still resides in him. It is late morning, approaching early Sunday afternoon. Social activity throughout town does not call to him. For its appeal can only bring distraction. His desire is to find inspiration for his art. Silent inspiration. Away from the bustling sounds of city life, and into the solitude of nature's gift for the downtrodden soul who begs for solace.

He arrives in the middle of nowhere. Somewhere on the outskirts of town but not too far away from civil existence. He looks up into nature's canvas of crystal blueness as it wraps itself around the greenery of trees. It is late summer. The natural lighting is different this time of year compared to the spring. The sun is more golden than yellow. This point of view is very keen to his artistic eye. Vibrant, and yet soft. Not knowing for sure if this is by design or happenstance. Beauty of sceneries mixed throughout the ages of things. The world is new. The world is maturated all at the same time.

Somehow through nature, through the silent atmosphere evolving around the core of his own spirit, Cidal searches for an idea to inspire his art. The amount of time sitting and meandering, wasting away watchful hours turn up no results. After having his fill of nothing more than fresh air, he leaves.

He returns to the city streets. Ongoing traffic on roads and sidewalks. People going about their business. An urge in his stomach for nutritious companionship. He stops in front of a small open door restaurant owned by a man old enough to be his father. The gentleman sits outside enjoying the warm weather.

"Hey, uncle," Cidal calls out to him. No blood relation, but out of respect to the older men of his race.

"Hello, sonny," the man responds back. "What's new?"

"Nothing. Just thought I stop in to fill my belly."

"Go on in. My servers will serve you."

"Thanks."

Cidal walks in, orders at the counter, and takes a seat at a table.

When close to being finished with his meal, the owner comes in and sits with him. He stares at Cidal with a look of satisfaction that his stomach is now content.

"Thanks, uncle. It hit all the right spots. The sight, smell, and taste. I'm full."

"You're very welcome."

"Nice Sunday afternoon."

"Ain't too bad."

"Kinda quiet in here, but busy out there."

"I reckon most folk went to church or something. They should be out. Now they can breathe."

Cidal laughs. "Why you say that? Don't you ever go?"

"I used to go many years back. I ain't got no use for it now."

"You don't believe in God?"

"I ain't said that. I just ain't got no use for church or church folk. That's all."

"I see. I gotcha."

"I don't see what big deal it is, no way. Folk make like if you don't step into a church and half fall asleep during the sermon, you going to the devil. Now that fella I don't believe in at all."

"Who? The devil?"

"Yeah, him. Folk go to church in fear of him instead of the love for God. If it wasn't for Satan, you wouldn't find a single soul in church. The devil keeps membership up, not God. Them members walk around scared every day of their lives. Once a crisis enter their lives, they butt-tail it, knocking down or running over anything that's in their way to get into somebody's church. When things are going good, you never see them sitting up in nobody's pew. It's basically a poor man's religion. The meek shall inherit the earth and all of that. Once they get a little money in their pocket, they gone. Bunch of hypocrites. You probably mad I'm telling you all of this."

"No, sir. I've never been in one myself."

"You never been to church?"

"Never."

"Hmm…you look like the type that would."

"Would what?"

"Would go to church."

"Strictly orphan. Never had any parents."

"That so?"

"Yes, sir. I go my way by myself."

"Never been married?"

"No."

"You ain't missin' nothing. It's better you keep walking alone."

"But I want to get married."

"For what?"

"To share my life with someone."

"Hogwash! Bunch of foolishness."

"I see you have never been married."

"Oh, yes I have. That's why I can tell you to avoid it at all cost. It don't enhance a man's life at all. Only brings us down. You no longer belong to yourself. Your thoughts, your actions is always wrong according to them."

"According to who?"

"Wives…women…it's all the same. And forget discussing anything with them. You will never win any arguments no matter how logical you are. We men are practical. We use reason. I don't know what them women use. It definitely ain't what we got."

"How long were you married?"

"Too long. I lost count. One single day is way too long in my book."

"Maybe it'll be different with me."

"I thought the same thing once. And look what happened. How old is you anyway?"

"45."

"If you made it this long, you really don't need it."

"I want to be married. I need to be."

"You need to be? Listen here, son. No man needs to be married. All you thinking about is the free sex. Well, there's price to pay for that. And let me tell you another thing. A man's sex life takes a nosedive after marriage. Oh, yeah, the wife may give in every once in a while just to keep us from pestering them. It ain't never enough. Mark my word. I speak the truth."

"But how can that be?"

"I know. It ain't logical. No sound reasoning can come from it. But you got to look at who we're dealing with too. Logic and anything that's common sense goes out with the slop pail. Don't get me wrong. I ain't got nothing against women. They can do whatever they want. Even be president of America. My beef is in being married."

"I gotcha, sir."

Never argumentative, Cidal takes the philosophy of others in stride. He asks points of why they feel about certain things instead of fighting against what they believe. Then, he is able to see their light. Their viewpoint. All without raising one single voice of opposition. He holds silent to what he truly feels and believes in. His struggles are not or have ever been with external forces. Internal conflict drives wedges within his own paradigm. Others he can walk away from, if he chooses to. But he cannot escape his own psyche.

Stepping outside of the restaurant, Cidal takes in a deep fresh breath. Like sand filled shoes, he moves across the paved sideway in no rush to get anywhere fast. Hands in his pockets, he eyes his steps ten paces in front. His vision focuses on the ground in his future path, moving to the left or right of oncoming pedestrians, motorbikes, and one or two stray dogs. Maybe even a scurrying cat.

Always observant because of his nature and his art, he does the opposite and takes on a role of someone who has had enough of the finer or ills of this life. Without the recognition of anything outwardly, the broth of his soul, mind, and heart cooks in the same kettle. He retreats back home to his living… *almost death*…quarters. Climbs the stairs to the second floor, turns the key in the keyhole, he hears a voice.

"I still want my money by the end of the week like I said."

Cidal turns just before he opens the door, cascading his eyes downstairs where Ms. Pearly stands.

"I will," he says. "Don't worry."

"I mean it."

"Sure you do. I mean it too." He enters his apartment and closes the door behind him.

3

Restlessness overtakes his mind. He tries to focus on art, but still cannot seem to find an idea of what he is searching for. On canvas, he makes drawings. Special colors of paint are made from old school style. Cidal does not use chemical paint which is common among modern artists. He has researched and found what works best for him, and to give him a touch of ancient creativity. Flowers, milk, and gum are his technique for mixing. As a result of this, colors will last and brings vividness to his portraits. Even some of his darker mood paintings leaning against the wall using dark colors have its own brightness. The mood of death can also bring light to the ones who desire it. His frustration leads him to abandon what he cannot finish. At least for the present time.

He grabs from the kitchen a bottle of high spirits and a shot glass. He walks it over to his laptop computer setting on the kitchen table. It is open to a particular website.

For the past six to nine months, Cidal has convinced himself that he needs a certain type of woman to be his soul mate. He has dated women within the stars and stripes of the country most of his adult life. Regardless of hue, skin-tone, or ethnicity, he has tried his lack of luck with several, but was unable to completely connect to his finding. More often he is not the idea type of what women are looking for rather than the reverse. Every situation with each woman, she would lay down her reasons of why their match is far from perfect.

Instead of sitting around and sulking for something that might have been, Cidal is quick to draw the curtains on unsuccessful relationships. It is neither his loss nor theirs. There is no real loss at all, according to his mindset. Some last. Some don't. Each interaction is precious within itself. Again, his battle is never with others. A knot of rope pulls in the opposite direction within him.

His search for what he thinks he wants in a future wife he hopes to find on China Romance Select. This website is filled with women from China who are taking their search for a husband across national borders to broaden their horizons for a chance of intercultural romance and marriage. Most women on this site feel they have been passed over by the men of their country, so they are willing to open themselves to men outside of China. However, there are many who still prefer a husband from within their borders. This website makes it easier to connect with them.

Throughout the six to nine months that Cidal has been sorting out potential mates, he has discovered many are not interested in his profile. He has three to four photos of himself and a description of his interests, hobbies, and what he desires in a future mate. He sends out messages or heart interest to many different women, and to his dismay, they return nothing back to him. He has read many testimonials about how many of the western men have their incoming mailboxes flooded with responses from women or the women's initiation to contact the men. No one has ever initiated interest to him. Nor have they ever responded to his pursuit of them. He is indeed a western man. A western man even from American. But maybe the wrong type of western man. Not one who is in the majority. But a minority candidate. Someone who is quickly passed over.

Checking the incoming box of interest or messages, it remains empty. There is a feature to see if anyone has even looked at his profile. His face remains untouched. His messages unexplored.

'Nothing,' he says to himself. 'I don't know how much longer I'll keep doing this. If I can at least get one woman's interest, I'll be on my way to starting something.'

He scans more profiles. He sends out two or three messages to newer members on the website. He can only wait to see if his luck will turn for his betterment. Enough is enough. He logs off and shuts the computer down, closing his laptop. Nothing is promised. He downs one to two shots of liquor.

There is need for another kind of companionship. One to relieve stress…anxiety…to make him complete and satisfied of all natural urges. Cidal has no woman friend. No one to turn to when his desires run high. In order to quench his rising tendencies, he has to resort to the oldest profession for his fulfillment.

Through his mobile device, he looks up a familiar and well known website for escort companionship. Many local women who advertise their services around the outskirts of Rising Falls, but they also may be closer to the major metropolitan city. And there are traveling escorts who come into town for however long, and then they are off to their next destination. Most are independent, working for and with no one else but themselves.

Cidal runs across an ad that features Asian escorts who have just arrived in town. Photos look too good to be true. Professionally done. Or models of another type. Maybe just enough to whet the appetite to get men calling and knocking on their door. This is not his first time calling on services for companionship, but his first to call upon an Asian agency. He uses search engine to look up the number before calling to make sure they are legitimate. He gets his answer and makes a call.

A woman with an Asian accent answers.

> *Hello, how are you?*
> *Yes, I would like to make an appointment.*
> *Hour or half-hour, sir?*
> *One hour.*
> *Okay, what time come?*
> *In 20 minutes.*
> *Okay, I'll text you address and price.*
> *Okay.*
> *Call when you arrive.*
> *Okay.*
> *Bye.*
> *Good-bye.*

He ends the call. Seconds later, he gets a text message from the agency of the location of the hotel and price for an hour worth of time and companionship. He quickly cleans up, brushes his teeth, tightens up his casual wear, touches of his favorite cologne in all the right places, makes certain his cash is sufficient which he slips inside a small white envelope, and then he leaves.

A special place is set aside for parking of motorbikes while other parking is reserve for automobiles and other vehicles. Cidal takes a deep breath and calls.

> *Hello, you calling for appointment? The same woman asks*
> *when she picks the phone.*
> *I'm here for my appointment.*
> *Okay, very good. Room number 1-2-8.*
> *128…okay.*
> *Thank you.*

Cidal knows the photos of the escort ad will not be any resemblance of who he will meet behind the closed door. However, he has a preference for Asian women. So what he gets, he will not complain about. Also, the woman on the phone will not be who he will meet. This is understood as well. She is only a scheduler for appointments. Most often in these scenarios, the scheduler will know more English than whatever girl he will meet. So says the clients who have reviewed this particular agency. He knows what to expect and what not to. All will be an adventure.

To participate in this kind of hobby, Cidal is aware of the potential danger it brings. The most important is law enforcement stings. There are certain signs to lookout for if the appointment will end up with a police being in the room for a bust. He is very fortunate enough never to have been caught up in some random operation of blue uniforms with too much time on their hands. Reading advice from reviewers on escort sites, doing his own research to know the rules of play, and what rights one has if ever stuck in a situation where officers are rounding up "johns" and packing them into patrol wagons like sardines. He has done his homework. But he also knows that it can happen to him at any appointment when he is not familiar with a particular woman for services.

He sees two young Asian women walking on the hotel grounds talking among themselves. His thoughts---they could be escorts. Picking up on the language, it appears to be Mandarin. He is quick to notice the Chinese language by words and tones. The two young women are reasonably attractive. This gives him hope of connecting with a girl of like characteristics.

Standing in front of room 128, Cidal knocks not too soft, not too hard and waits. This is the part he hates the most. The anticipation…not the appearance of the female. Getting his foot in the door, knowing there is no sting operation working against him is his only thought. Anything else he can handle. Twenty seconds which feels like twenty minutes, the door opens slowly.

Peering from behind the door is a semi-shy young Chinese woman.

4

From what he knows, he greets her immediately in her language.

"Ni hao." Which means hello.

"Ni hao," she answers back. "You are handsome."

"Thank you. You're cute yourself."

She is not overly attractive. Often by most people's stereotype of what Asian women in her profession should look like. An average to a pleasant appearance; tilting on the brink of almost being pretty when light strikes her at a certain angle or viewed from a distance. Her height and weight is very proportional for women of her culture. No more than 5'4. Around 110 pounds at best. From head-to-toe, her proportions evenly match up.

He steps inside the room and she closes the door. He gives her a hug. She receives it warmly. He looks around, trying to pick up if anything was out of the ordinary. He thinks of creating an excuse to check the bathroom by wanting to wash his hands. To make sure law or any other enforcer is not behind the shower curtain. This notion is quickly dispelled. So natural is her demeanor, he is at ease instantly. Amazed at his attempt at Mandarin, she could not help to ask...

"You speak-uh Chinese?" Her Chinese accent is very broken speaking English.

"No, just a couple of words here and there." She seems to understand him. "You speak English?" he asks.

"I speak-uh English some. More than I work with girls."

He understands this to mean *more than with the girls she works with.*

"What is your name?" he asks.

"My name…Wei Mei."

"Oh, my name is Cidal."

Without question, she accepts his unusual name. "Nice to meet you."

"Nice to meet you, too, Wei Mei. Is that your escort or real name?"

"You find out you nice enough."

He chuckles and agrees with the arrangement.

Out of his pocket, he pulls an envelope and gently places it on the dresser. She is puzzled. He smiles.

"This is for you," he says.

"This what?" she asks.

She picks up the envelope and takes out the money. "Ahh…" She acknowledges his very classy way of presenting her with the donation. "I like. Very nice style."

No rush is required. There is a whole hour in front of them. A physical embrace he performs, because he cannot keep his arms from being around her quiet sensuousness. Her disposition is very subtle. Nothing about her cries out for attention or screams of sexuality. She could walk the streets of any Chinatown and would never turn one head. Her aura attracts from within. Her tender behavior. The softness of her voice.

By hand, she escorts him to the side of the bed where he sits. She kneels to unlace his shoes and carefully pulls them off. He raises her to her feet in appreciation, hugs, and begins to kiss her. She controls the tempo of their action. No flinging off clothes like two teenage sex fiends unable to sustain passion from within or a typical westerner who has an uncontrolled desire or a certain flair for a typical color of fever. Slowly, undressing him by her delicate hand takes place.

"I give you massage," she says.

"Okay. Sounds good."

He is in his natural. Her uncovering first begins with her breasts and private area, and then she releases the rest of her clothing to match his naturalness. Smoothness of her feminine touch, she rubs unscented oil from China as she begins her technique of soothing every pore of his physique. Twenty to twenty-five minutes of a whole body massage from the back to the front.

"Western woman like fast sex," she says. "No, no, no. Chinese woman take time best for sex."

As he moans with every soft rub and stroke of her hands, "I agree," he admits.

Her tendency evolves around the passion of her tight intimacy. The nature of her culture welcomes him into her civilization. The center of her universe propels him to explore other galaxies. Generation after generation…lightyears upon lightyears…breaks everything down into moments…into seconds…one drop at pinpoint tip…they return back into the present time.

Fifteen to twenty minutes remain on his hour. Lying close in girlfriend experience, they hold each other with light conversation. Cidal has his mobile phone next to him for translation purposes in case.

"You good lover. I like," she says.

"I like you, too, Mei Wei."

"Wei Mei. No, Mei Wei."

"Sorry."

"In China, family name first, given name last."

"Oh, I see. So this is your real name?"

"I did not tell."

"Your English is not bad."

"I study little. I work with girls, know no English."

"Ahh…"

"English hard for Chinese learn."

"Yes, I can imagine. The two languages are so different."

"What you say?"

"The two languages are so different."

"I don't know."

"You don't know what?"

"I don't understand."

Cidal gets on his mobile and pushes translation app. English into Chinese. He repeats what he said previously into the speaker part of his phone. On the screen, it has the English wording, and just below the line, the Chinese characters along with voice translation.

"Oh, I understand now," she says. "I like." Referring to the app on his phone.

"It's good to have."

"I get one on my phone."

"That would be good. Especially, in your business."

"American know no Chinese?"

"No. Maybe Chinese-Americans do."

"Oh."

"What part of China are you from?"

"Shanghai."

"That's great."

"You come China and visit? Shanghai? I show you."

"Wonderful."

"Really? When you come?"

"I don't know. I have to sell some paintings to pay for the trip."

"Paintings?"

"Yes. I'm an artist…I paint portraits."

"Oh, very good. I like."

"You like art?"

"Yes, I like very much."

"I'll have to show you some of my work sometime."

"I like."

"How long will you be here?"

"I don't know. Up to boss." She holds up two fingers. Then one finger.

"Two what?"

"Maybe two weeks. One month. I don't know."

"How long have you been in America?"

"Three weeks."

"Straight here to Rising Falls?"

"No, first New York."

"Okay, and then here?"

"Yes, that's right."

"You like America?"

There is no answer. She looks at him. He waits to hear. She does not look at him anymore.

"I don't know," she says. "I will see."

"How old are you?"

"30."

"Really? You don't look like it."

"How old I look?"

"Around 20 or 21 maybe."

"Oh."

"You married?"

She looks at him as though he has three eyes.

"Okay, stupid question," he says. "Do you have a boy-friend?"

"No. You married?"

"No."

"What your age?"

"Guess."

"35."

"No, thanks. 45."

"45? You no look."

"Thanks."

"You younger look."

Killing more time, it is obvious they are enjoying the other's conversation. Her phone rings. She reaches to grab it from the nightstand beside the bed.

"Boss."

Wei Mei speaks on the phone at the same time as she is getting up. Her whole conversation is in Chinese. Cidal lies there and marvels over the spoken language of Mandarin. It sounds so strange and beautiful simultaneously. After ending the call with her boss, she glances at him with disappointment.

"Our time up."

"Aww...that's too bad," he says. He does not want to overstay his welcome. He gets up and starts to dress; she puts on her bra and panties. She, being the lady that she is, sits him down on the side of the bed as she kneels to put on his shoes, tying his laces back up. He hugs her, missing her already before even stepping out of the door.

"You come back?" she asks.

"I want to come and see you again," he says. "When my money is right."

"I don't understand."

"It's nothing. I really want to. Will you leave before I come back?"

"Maybe not. I don't know."

"I need to communicate with you."

"You have WeChat?"

"No. What's WeChat?"

On her phone, Wei Mei shows him the app. It is a Chinese app for social networking. She takes his phone and instructs him how to apply it to his phone. With username, WeChat ID, and all, she demonstrates to him how to send her a message so she can accept his invitation to become WeChat friends. In no time, they are now free to communicate with each other. She accepts his invitation to become one of her circle of friends. She messages him back. It is all in Chinese characters. Instead of always holding the message dialogue on the screen so the text messages can translate from Chinese to English, she sets it up so it automatically translate on its own whenever she sends a message to him. They are connected. He can check on her. She can contact him if her plans change to leave town sooner than expected.

A short silk robe she slips on her to be presentable when escorting him to the door. One last hug. One last kiss. Turning away, Cidal looks back at her before opening the door.

"I will see you again," he says.

"I happy you do."

5

No sense in fooling himself. His art is not good enough to support his living. In fact, his art is good enough, because good art is not predicated on how much it sells for. Bad art, if there is such a thing, can sell thousands or even millions of dollars. Not because of the quality of the art piece. It depends on who is willing to pay what price. Older pieces, people pay a higher price. If particular pieces are in possession of a well-known or a famous person, they pay a higher price. An artist throws something, anything together, possibly a higher price is paid for. An unknown, no name, struggling, but a very good artist, a lower price will be paid for his work, if paid for at all.

Cidal has sold pieces not consistent enough to rely on this for his bread-n-butter. This is why he hits the alarm clock every Monday through Friday morning, working the first shift at the Rising Falls Memorial Hospital keeping bathrooms, hallways, lobbies, and much of everything else clean. Pushing floor dusters and rolling mop buckets around; maintaining spotless counters and desktops; no smudges on mirrors or windows; trash bins emptied with new, fresh bags. In places like medical facilities, no dirt can be seen or spotted with a white glove inspection regardless of how high or low the area of cleaning is.

His practical plan is to pay his rent at the end of the week. His pay check will be handed to him at the end of his shift come Friday afternoon. Though economical is his living arrangements, it is still more than the price of paid companionship late Sunday evening. Being a man with desires not met by any woman, he feels a need to slightly splurge to balance mind, soul, and body. Also, he knows he cannot spend whenever the nature of manhood surges onto the battlefield of passion to awaken his loins because his purse strings will not allow it. Working within him, there is a force that is greater than what occasionally protrudes below his navel.

Casual slacks, wearing a polo shirt inscription signifies which department in the Rising Falls Memorial Hospital he works in; however, this is covered up by the light blue scrubs he and other cleaning crew members have to wear. A V-neck short-sleeve shirt with a drawstring pants. Cidal stands and stares into space while briefly stopping his mopping duties. Thoughts come across his mind of an earlier circumstance.

Just before daybreak, when night is still fighting not to lose its clout with the dawning of the upcoming hours; a loud sound of an eagle screech opens Cidal's eyes. Not in panic. But casually, as though nothing in this world could ever take him by surprise. Lying in bed on his side, he feels the presence of something looming over him. Taking his time to change positions, he turns over onto his back. He rubs his eyes and sits up.

A woman stands at the foot of the bed glaring at him, wearing no certain expression. Her countenance makes it difficult to decipher if her intentions are well or ill. Her attire is of a long gown; her age is hard to pinpoint on mere observation. She brings years of the opposite ends of a spectrum into one appearance. He is barely startled. His behavior is as if this occurrence happens regularly. Cidal inquires to find answers from his intruder who has crept into his room without an invitation.

"Who are you?" he asks. "And how did you get in here?"

I am Mother Goddess. All I have to do is appear.

Cidal shakes his head in disbelief and refocuses his eyes. What he sees is indeed for real.

"Who? What kinda of game is this?"

This is no game. I am who I say. You are not hallucinating. You see me in the flesh. But I am no longer of this world.

"What do you mean by that?"

In earthly terms, I am dead. I live on in spirit. This is what you see.

"You said you are some sort of Goddess. Why come to me?"

I come to you because of two reasons. I am your Goddess Mother. I had given birth to you 45 years ago.

"You're kidding? I can see you as clear as day. You can't be any spirit."

To prove if his scientific calculation is correct, Cidal grabs his pillow and tosses it at her. It goes right through and lands on the floor behind her. Her form, her physical appearance did not alter. He is flabbergasted, but not too much beyond his own disbelief.

"This can't be real. I must be dreaming."

You are not dreaming.

"Then why did you desert me?"

Some women can desert their own child, but a true mother cannot.

"Why show yourself to me now? All of those years I needed to see and hear you. I felt lonely and forgotten."

This brings up reason number two. Those who are still in earthly form can sometimes see beyond what is natural. When people are close to death, this physical world opens their souls to spiritual beings.

"So you're saying I'm close to death?"

Several hours ago, you were knocking on the door of eternity. The door opens, but you did not walk through. If your ceiling structure was more secure, you would have made it. You were dead for seconds before crashing back into your reality. Now you walk one thin line between two extremes. Standing on top of a hill, you can now view what is on both sides. Your steps are of both worlds.

The nightstand clock shoots off its ring like a fire alarm which redirects Cidal's attention. He turns it off and looks back at the foot of his bed. She is gone.

'Hmm…maybe this proves I wasn't dreaming,' he says to himself.

"Come again," a voice from behind rings out.

Cidal snaps out of his mesmerizing remembrance, his mop handle still in hand, turns his head to see his manager standing slightly behind him. A middle-aged, African-American woman dressed professionally, who chooses to don the style of her natural hair, which is nicely done, as oppose to the typical hairstyles of most women of her race. She does her job well and takes it seriously. Meaning, there are those who like her and those who don't.

"Oh, I'm sorry," Cidal apologizes. "I was thinking."

"Correction," his manager says. "This means you were dreaming. Daydreaming I believe they call it."

"I admit I was. I'll get back to my duties."

"I've been watching you lately. I know things are not quite right with you."

"I'm okay."

"I can see that you're not." She glances at her watch. "At 10:30, I would like to see you in my office." She walks away without waiting for a response.

Cidal continues to work. Ten minutes goes by, a dink notification from his mobile sounds. He slides to open the screen homepage and sees one message indication on his WeChat app. He pushes to view the text chat message left by Wei Mei. She states a question, and then he responds to it. They go back and forth.

> *What you doing?*
> *Working.*
> *Painting?*
> *No, my other job.*
> *Oh, I won't bother you.*
> *No, bother.*
> *You continue work. I miss you.*
> *I miss you too. I'll chat on my break.*
> *Ok*

Cidal walks into his manager's office exactly at 10:30. She sits behind her desk and directs him to sit. She is not one for idle small talk. Figuratively, her sleeves are rolled up; here comes a boxing glove punch right between his eyes.

"I think you're suffering from some mental or personal problems," she says. "Which one is it?'

"There's nothing wrong..."

Before he can finish his statement, she stops him cold.

"Cidal! There is no need to deny your condition. When you started working here ten months ago, your work was in tiptop order. Recently, you have been slagging behind not only in your duties, but in every phase while on company time. You take extended and more breaks than you are allowed to have. Your behavior has been sporadic also. One minute, you're Mr. Personality, and the next thing we know, you're down under digging graves. You have been calling off more than you should. I believe this will lead into something more dangerous. I'm not going to ask you if my diagnosis of you is correct, because I'm certain that it is."

She pulls out a business card from her desk and scribbles on the back it. She hands it to him.

"I want you to go see Dr. Madglove. He is well known in his field of psychiatry. From what I can observe, you have symptoms of early depression. I say early, because you weren't always like this."

"So, Luella, you want me to see some shrink? We don't see shrinks. I'm perfectly fine. Just lots of things going on with me. Nothing to be alarmed about."

"They all say that. You're in denial. I had someone in my family just like you. Besides, a shrink is not a good term to use. Professional help is what you need. I expect you to make the call. If not, I'll put you on absence leave. So I suggest you get it together and make a call to Dr. Madglove. There is no further discussion. You can go back to work now."

Mother Goddess appears, standing next to his manager, Luella. She speaks to Cidal.

You know she's right. You do need to get some sort of help. Your brain is tilted off its axis. It runs in our family. Most recently, your father.

Her appearance is so real and solid that Cidal forgets himself and responds.

"Is that so, Mother Goddess? You could've told me about that sooner. Like this morning."

Luella glares at him sternly. "What did you say? And what did you call me? If this is your way of being sarcastic or disrespectful, I can write you a pink slip and dismiss you from your job immediately."

"No, I'm sorry. Something came over me. I don't know what it was. It's nothing. Sorry."

Cidal's eyes are still staring at Mother Goddess. She shakes her head slowly in a non-affirmative way. Luella looks beside her, in direction of where Cidal's eyes are fixed. She sees nothing and looks back at him.

"You don't see what I see?" he asks his manager.

"And what do you see other than office fixtures?" she asks. "You better make that appointment with Dr. Madglove sooner than later. You will be the better for it."

Mother Goddess, very still in her motion, looks on.

He closes the door as soon as he steps out of the office. Checking out the business card for Dr. Madglove, Cidal speaks to himself. 'Great! A crackpot! I'm more insane for going to see him than not. The way I see it, no one was ever mentally insane before these types of doctors hung out their shingles. Then, they diagnosed anyone who shows that they're a normal human being within themselves as someone who's crazy to everyone else. Prostitutes do better for men's state of mind than these loonies. Dr. Madglove. He's definitely got the right name.'

His first two steps heading down the hall, two nurses start to pick up their pace, eyeing him cautiously when they had originally slowed down to observe Cidal talking to himself. To him, nothing is ever out of the ordinary. He continues his destination back to his duties.

6

Up to this point, his quality of life has been an oxymoron. External ice, internal fire. Outwardly a calm sea, inwardly a raging hurricane. Outside of himself, the surroundings of people everywhere. Inside of his physicality, an abandon air of loneliness. Bright and colorful are his paintings on the outer surface, while his inner cave consistently looms of an overcast gloom. His sheepish demeanor sometimes has a roar of a lion. Love of everything natural, and yet, he highly dislikes himself. But the only way to get out of his skin is to eliminate its shell…its outer covering…the temple of where his soul temporarily lives.

It is uncertain where his fate will end. Whatever moves him in one direction, in one moment, will use the same amount of force to pull him in another direction. His life is one breath, one step after another, a void of future thoughts. Like a swirling wind, he changes his outlook. His stability is never anchored no matter how positive or negative circumstances appear. One soul possesses many minds. His inner sea rocks his boat tumultuously while providing a face of no commotion.

'I have to create my masterpiece,' Cidal says to himself, getting up from his painting canvas to walk away. 'Not for worldly recognition, but for myself. I can't seem to get there.'

After working hours cleaning at the hospital, this is how he spends his evenings. Drawing with delicate precision; the stroke of a paint brush. Other times, he dabbles in abstract creativity to bring uniqueness to an art form that no other eyes see but his. He knows one simple painting brings with it one thousand eyes. No one sees the same image in the same way.

To help refocus, to sooth his mind, instead of pounding liquid high spirits, he decides to send a WeChat message to Wei Mei. Sweet. Short. Direct.

Hey! I miss you!

Surprisingly, she WeChat a message back within four minutes.

I miss you too. Come see me.

Knowing this would require some money, Cidal hesitates in responding. 'Man, what can I say to her? I've already dropped money two nights ago to see her. I gotta pay my rent when I get paid on Friday.'

He is smart enough to realize she wants to be paid for a visit. From one encounter with her, there is no way that she means to grant him any personal favors. It is all about business. Not relationship.

'I'm not sugarcoating nothing.' He sends back a message.

I would. But short on cash. Maybe when I have some extra money I will.

The game is too familiar to him. He is not going to wait around for a response. If this is no big deal to her, it definitely should not be all that important to him. He changes his mind. He goes into the kitchen, pours from bottle to glass, and pounds one shot down in one gulp. He dismisses thoughts of her in his mind. Never a notice or a mere thought of her lack of response comes to him. He preoccupies himself in his inner turmoil.

'Anytime I need a quick release I have to pay for it,' he says aloud. 'Ridiculous! I need something I don't have to pay for. At my age, if I don't use it regularly, I will definitely lose it. There has to be some woman I can abide my time with while waiting for my perfect match. Maybe some unhappily married woman, a younger woman, or some attractive middle-aged woman who feels no one desires her anymore. I need something.'

His mind needs refreshing. A concept…an idea he is still searching for to create his next portrait. The evening is still in daylight when he glances out of the window. He escapes.

A nice stroll without hurry; hands inside pockets; people are out socializing or attending to their business, Cidal goes to Garden Square, a park in the center of town, and finds a group of people from the younger to the more matured, dancing to music from a past era. The sounds of 1920's, 30's, or 40's, maybe. Black singers and musicians records are being played. No fancy costumes or clothing of the musical time. Come as you are. Others sit and watch. While Cidal stands and observes, a vibrating and slight ding of his mobile phone goes off in his pocket. His WeChat app indicates a message. He opens it.

Sorry, I with visitors. Free now.

Being surprised by her returned message, his hopes heighten but not too much. He remembers who he is by past experiences. A half-second zing of expectations flattens back to the ground without too far of a fall. His desire is to see her regardless of his lack of funds. There is nothing to hold back; nothing to be overly concerned about; absolutely nothing to fear, because he has already stared down death in its eyes. Anything living is not even close to an afterthought. He sends a message to her. They correspond.

> *How long will you be free?*
> *Don't know. Whatever boss tell.*
> *I will come after your appointments.*
> *You not come now?*
> *I'm not going through your boss to see you. I'm dealing with*
>   *you and no one else.*
> *Ok.*

"How goes it?" a voice from behind asks.

Cidal turns to see who is addressing him. A dark skin man of unknown age glares at him with a crazed look in his eyes but smiling.

"Hi," Cidal replies, not recognizing him.

"That's all you got for me?"

"That's all of what?"

"You know, man. Just hi and that's it?"

"I'm sorry. I can't place you."

"You placing me right here."

"Right here?"

"Yeah, man. I stands in front of you. Placed right here."

"I mean I don't seem to know you."

"Recognize, recognize," he says, smiling, still with a crazed look in his eyes. "You do know, but you don't recognize."

"I'm sorry. I don't."

"I thought so."

"But you look familiar."

"Man, don't come off with that. I knows you don't recognize."

"What's your name?"

"Blue Beans…that's what I'm called."

"I don't place your name."

"There you goes again misplacing stuff. I said Blue Beans."

"I don't remember any Blue Beans."

Daunting as he looks with his glare of unpredictability, his half smile sets off anything threatening. Cidal tries to remember by studying his face. Eventually, he extends his hand.

"Well, my name is…"

Blue Beans pushes Cidal's hand away. "Don't bother. I already knows who you is."

"Who am I, then?" Cidal asks.

"Sui."

"Sui?"

"Yeah, that's who you is. See, I recognize you."

"What do you mean, Sui?'

"Get it. Sui…Suicide…Sui-Cidal… Suicidal. Cidal for short. That's you. And folks think I'm crazy."

This leaves Cidal speakless. They have a competitive stare down. This time Blue Beans has no smile. Now, his looks and what he knows about Cidal becomes intimidating. Too many people around to be too dangerous of what could happen. The music beckons a call to the ear of Blue Beans.

"I gots to get my dance on." He walks away. He goes to the middle of the gathering, claps his hands one loud time to start his awkward, ungraceful moves with those crazed eyes and a huge, crooked smile.

Perplexing as the situation is, Cidal can do nothing but look on.

7

Wei Mei is having a conversation with one of her coworkers in their Chinese language inside her hotel room. The two women engage in light-spirited dialogue about the clientele of Rising Falls compared to other places they have been. Xia, her coworker friend, prefers the big city life and clients, while Wei Mei is getting adjusted to towns that are not as fashionable. Hometown men seem to be more respectful and appreciative than the high-rollers, take women for granted, big city phalluses, according to Wei Mei. However, Xia salivates for those slickers with longer arms and deeper pockets.

The WeChat app signals a message from her mobile, bringing pause to their talk time. Wei Mei retrieves her phone and sees that it is from Cidal. She lets Xia knows who it is. A client she has seen once before. The hotel room digital clock reads 11:30 pm. Usually, their appointments stop at around 11:00 every night. Therefore, this goes beyond what is expected. Especially, if the regular protocol is not followed in the setting up of appointments. This also indicates that if clients are seen without the boss knowing about it, this may not be looked upon as too favorable, because the boss will be left out of the exchanging of funds. Quite simply, the boss will not get a share of the money. The boss wants to know all that goes on with all of the girls. Occasionally, there are some exceptions.

Xia asks Wei Mei what she will do in Chinese. Her calm, but clueless expression says it all. On the spur of the moment, Wei Mei quickly sends back a reply. In the process in getting out of her on what she had decided, Xia bombards her friend with questions to no avail.

A single loud knock on the door. Without delay, Wei Mei goes to the door, peeks out of the peephole, and then opens it. Cidal appears.

"How are you?" she greets.

"Fine," he replies.

He is whisked in by Wei Mei. She closes the door softly.

"My friend, Xia, this is," Wei Mei introduces.

"Hello, Xia. I'm Cidal."

"She no English," Wei Mei explains to Cidal as Xia stands without dialogue, but with a welcoming smile.

"Ni hao," Cidal greets her again in Chinese.

This time she returns a greeting of, "Ni hao," back to him. Short, direct dialogue between the two ladies has Xia excusing herself, so Wei Mei and her gentleman caller can have their privacy. Once her friend is out of the room, Wei Mei locks the door and turns to Cidal.

"You see me again. Very happy."

"Yes, I wanted to."

She walks towards him; they embrace. They kiss. Then she remembers…holding out her hand…

"You have envelope?"

Cidal knows exactly what she is referring to. "No, I don't. No envelope this time. I wanted to see you. We won't be engaging tonight."

"No envelope?"

"No."

"You don't like?"

"Yes, I like you. I'm short of cash."

"What to do?"

"I won't ask you for any special favors. Just talk." He escorts her by her arm to the side of the bed where they both sit. "Is that okay?"

"Okay. No more visitors today."

"No more visitors?"

"No appointment."

"Oh."

"My boss may call and check."

"Really?"

"Maybe."

"You still don't know how long you'll be here?"

"Don't know how long. Maybe two weeks. Maybe month or more. I don't know."

"How is business?"

"Okay. As American say, not bad."

"Would you like to go out to eat with me before you go?"

"You Chinese restaurant here?"

"Yes. The Golden Bowl."

"That's wonderful. I may not to go."

"Why not?"

"Boss may not let. I will see.

"Couldn't you sneak away sometimes?"

"No, no, no. Boss no like."

"Does your boss have to know?"

She does not say anything but looks deeply into his eyes. He lets her. He has no plans of interrupting her. She touches his cheek.

"Who you are?" she asks.

Nothing comes to Cidal's mind for a response. Silence is best when there is no obvious answer. She understands his lack of words.

"I know," she says finally. "You don't know."

"How do you know? Are you a psychic?"

"No."

"Christian?"

"Noooo...that's worse."

"You believe in anything?"

"Confucius thought."

"Hmm...smart girl. Very practical. Common sense. No pie-in-the-sky theology."

"What you say? I don't understand."

"I like."

"You like?"

"Your style."

"You don't know who you are. Very good."

An impulse takes over and Cidal swoops forward for a kiss on Wei Mei's lips. She does not refuse. He does it again. Still, no refusal. Third round he goes for a passionate press of her lips, wrapping his arms around her with a tight embrace. They slowly allow themselves to fall gently on the bed, lips continuously locked. A soft landing in the middle of the bed brings out laughter from her. A sweet, feminine laughter.

"What's funny?" he asks.

"Envelope?" she says.

"Can I lay with you? I won't do anything."

They position themselves in the center of the bed. Lying on their sides. Face-to-face.

"I must sleep-uh. I long day."

"I won't keep you long, Wei Mei."

"You are beast…I can tell."

"Me? A beast?"

"Beast inside. Sheep on outside."

"I'll show you beast."

He moves in with a kiss of high sensuality. She laughs and playfully pushes him away. He rolls to the side of the bed and allows himself to cascade to the floor.

PLOP!

Cidal opens his eyes. To his amazement, he is no longer in the hotel room in the late of night with Wei Mei. It is daylight. He sits up from the floor of his own bedroom in his pajamas. He shakes his head in disbelief. He shoots a sharp glance at the nightstand clock. 11:30 am.

'What! I couldn't have been dreaming. It was too real.' Then he remembers. 'Work! I'm late for work.'

He jumps up. His mobile rings. He sees that it is his work number. He answers right away to explain he had overslept.

"Hello!"

"Finally!" a female voice speaks on the other end. "Where have you been?"

"I'm sorry, Luella. I must have overslept. I'll be in as soon as I get dress."

"Nonsense! Three days!"

"What? Three days? What do you mean?"

"Are you drunk or high on something?"

"No!"

"It's been three days since you last reported to work."

"What?"

"Don't act like you don't know. Tuesday was the last day you showed up."

"No way! What day is it today?"

"Friday."

Suddenly, there is a pounding on the door of his apartment. Ms. Pearly makes her vocal impression.

"I know you're in there, you half-dazed buffoon! You know what day it is? I want my money!"

Still in his haze, Cidal ignores the pounding and the vocal tirade by plugging one ear with his finger while his phone is clamped to his other. A ceaseless beating and calling out, Ms. Pearly continues her verbal onslaught.

"These last couple of days you been avoiding me," she says. "Trying to lay low thinking I'll forget. But honey, I ain't forgot nothing! Especially when it comes to my money. I shoulda thrown you out months ago. We got folk around here who's looking for a place to stay, and here I am losing money because of you. I'll be jack-stick-it!"

Cidal speaks low into the phone to his manager.

"I'll be in as soon as I get dress."

"I'm trying to decide if I'm going to keep you on," Luella says.

"Please don't do anything until I see you. I can't explain what happened. I don't remember one thing."

"You have one hour to get here. If you don't, I will have to dismiss you from your position." She disconnects the call.

That irritating sound by drumming the door; those screeching words coming from the landlady's voice prompts Cidal to take flight like a soaring hawk as he rushes to the apartment door. He springs it open. Ms. Pearly's fist does not connect to door but almost knocks Cidal on the head. He stands, without a flinch in movement...unfazed by her accidental near right jab.

"I'll have your money later today," he snaps.

She gives him the once over look from head-to-toe. "You still in your night clothes? Ain't you going to work today?"

"I'm on my way if you can cut me some slack."

"Slack? That's all you been doing lately. You hiding. I know it. Ain't nobody seen or heard from you since early this week. You try to avoid paying your rent."

"It's not that. I just don't remember."

"Of course you don't. Most drunkards can't even remember their own names because being high off that liquor. You're a mess. All of you so-called artists are. Why even do it if you got to kill yourself doing it? Just let it go and find a decent job. Get married. But I don't know who would want you."

"I got to get ready."

Hearing enough bombardment over events he can't recall, Cidal closes the door quickly out of frustration, but quietly out of partial respect.

8

Coworkers give him a strange look, performing their cleaning duties. Cidal knows they are watching him as he walks through the hall heading towards the manager's office. He avoids direct eye contact, using his peripheral vision to spot them out. When he arrives at Luella's office, he stops before knocking, checks his watch…12:30…exactly one hour since he last spoke to her on the phone. He knocks.

"Come in," a female voice says.

He enters to see Luella standing behind her desk. She slowly sits and tells him to have a seat. He closes the door and takes her direction.

"I can't explain a thing," Cidal starts out. "And that's no lie. If I knew what happened, I would be frank about it. I haven't a clue."

"Abusing alcohol and drugs will do that to you," she says, half sarcastically. "It does funny things to your brain. Puts you in a partial coma. Makes you forget stuff."

"No, I'm serious."

"No, I'm serious in telling you that this is your last chance. You need help. Lots of help. Until you see Dr. Madglove, don't even think about coming back to work."

"It may take weeks to get an appointment from him."

"No, it wouldn't. Mention my name when you call. He'll take you when…" She pauses and picks up her mobile phone. "As matter of fact, I'll call him right now." Apparently, she has his number in her contact list. She scrolls to his name and presses to connect the call.

"Hello, Dr. Madglove. This is Luella. How soon are you available? I want to send one of my employees to come see you." She waits and listens. Cidal hears a man's voice on other end of the phone, but he cannot distinguish what is being said. "Okay. Perfect timing. He will be there soon. Thank you for the last minute acceptance. We'll talk soon. Bye." She disconnects the call, places her phone back on her desk, and stares at him.

"Maybe I don't want to go," Cidal says.

"Maybe or not does not matter. You need to go if you plan on continuing working here. 2:00 is your appointment. The address is on the business card I gave you. You can get yourself together and leave now."

Nothing more is said. Cidal gets up and leaves her office.

Her edges, at times, may be a little rough, but Cidal knows she wants what is best for him. Luella comes across as uncaring, a lack of concern, maybe even domineering over those who she manages over; however, Cidal can sense bits and pieces of kind-heartedness buried underneath her exterior surface.

Once he arrives at the psychiatrist's office, Cidal looks at the business card and building address to match the location of his destination. He walks inside the office where a receptionist sits at her desk.

"May I help you, sir?"

"Yes, I'm Cidal…"

"Oh, yes!" she exclaims, not giving him time to complete his introduction. "Dr. Madglove can't wait to meet…I mean Dr. Madglove is waiting for you in his office. He's expecting your case…I mean he's expecting you. Go right in."

"Thank you."

Knuckles in midair before connecting to the door, Cidal is stopped by the receptionist. "Oh, no bother doing that," she says. "Open the door and walk right in."

Half-way surprised by this, Cidal gives her a nod, turns the doorknob, and steps in.

A man stands with his back to Cidal, observing the natural lighting of a beautiful day outside of his office window. His hands are behind his back. From what Cidal can tell, he is man of African descent…probably not from Africa, but far removed from the continent by many generations. In other words, an African-American. He has a small, salt-n-peppered Afro, indicating his maturity and years of professional study.

"You may sit after you close the door," his distinguished voice sounds out.

Once Cidal closes the door and sits in a chair in front of the doctor's desk, he is redirected.

"No, my pet, in the recliner chair," Dr. Madglove commands with authority, never once turning around to face him.

Cidal looks around the room and spots an Easy boy recliner over to his far left on the other side of the office. He goes and sits. For the very first time, Dr. Madglove makes his facial appearance known. Wearing thin wired, silver glasses and the same mixture goatee that matches his small Afro. He eases over and takes a seat in a cushioned office furniture chair across from where Cidal is positioned. A glass round table is between them. A notepad and writing utensil sets on top. Dr. Madglove grabs it and crosses his legs. He studies Cidal without expression. Eyes piercing like lasers from his dark pupils. One minute. Maybe two goes by without a sound or a word. The arid communication finally finds rainfall with threats of an eventual downpour.

"Why are you here?" Dr. Madglove asks.

"Because I'm mad," Cidal replies. "Pardon my pun."

"This I can see. I felt it as you entered the room. No need for me to see your face to know what I'm dealing with. You are dealing with psychological and spiritual warfare. Your body is torn not knowing which side to take. These are reasons why ending your life is your best option. You have tried, I know. I felt it also as you entered. Depression is real. Male depression is worse. Men are expected to do and be so much. When men fail at their responsibility or duty, they feel they are not worthy of existence. Therefore, they become distracted, overturned by their inner turmoil of not being or having enough testosterone to be who they are meant to be. You are depressed and you do not even know it. You downplay the signs and symptoms. You resist mental health treatments. There is loss interest in work; feeling you cannot work or get things done; abusing alcohol or drugs to feel better or to lose yourself entirely; feeling restless or irritable; problems sleeping; out of focus and not remembering. And yes, my pet, even sexual inability."

"You used *my pet* twice. Why?"

"Because you and all of my patients are helpless pets that are crying out for attention and help. Some are soft kitty cats… others are dangerous cobras. I know which one you are. I know exactly where you lie."

Cidal has no questions on where he lies. There isn't one curiosity of thought concerning Dr. Madglove's opinion of his state of being or even how he came up with such an assessment. He holds steady. He does not and will not give into the prognosis of his mental state. To him, it does not matter. He has no interest in trying to find or figure out who he is. That is for people who actually care about who they are. He can take himself or leave himself.

"Allow me to continue," Dr. Madglove says. "Major depression is also known as unipolar or major depression disorder. It is characterized by a persistent feeling of sadness or a lack of interest in everything. Unipolar depression is solely focused on the 'lows' or the negative emotions and symptoms that one may be experiencing. MDD or Major Depressive Disorder. There are a few types. Let's focus on the two I think you may be dealing with. One is Psychotic Depression, which often develops if you have been hallucinating or you believe in delusions that are not cohesive with reality. This can be caused by a traumatic event or if you have already had a form of depression in the past. Two is Melancholy Depression, which often exhibits the most typical signs of depression including a decreased interest in activities one once loved. I wonder which one of the two better describes you."

Dr. Madglove sits in silence. He waits for his patient to respond. Cidal feels there is no question that was asked, so he continues to lounge waiting for the doctor's next soliloquy. Neither party is disturbed or uneasy with the lack of communication between each of them.

Suddenly, Mother Goddess makes her appearance at the table. She sits with her legs crossed as if positioning herself in an invisible chair. This gets Cidal's attention. This peaks Dr. Madglove's interest even though he is oblivious to her presence. He observes Cidal intently.

"Oh, it's you again," Cidal says to Mother Goddess.

Careful, careful. Remember, you are the one who is only allowed to see or hear me. The doctor already believes you are cracking up.

"Great," Cidal sighs. "He's gonna really think I've lost it now. Of all the times to show up…why now?"

So often, I have to check on my little boy.

"Your little boy needed you when he was just that. Now, he's a grown man. He's gotten along pretty well with no assistance."

I wouldn't call killing yourself getting along pretty well. Besides, I couldn't kill myself either. Situational drama prevented me from doing so.

"I didn't kill myself. I had changed my mind. I struggled, but I got free. And what situational drama kept you from raising me? You never did tell me before."

"This is incredible," Dr. Madglove says out loud, awestruck on the apparent conversation his patient is engaging with himself. He scribbles notes in his notepad, constantly keeping a close eye on his subject. The person who Cidal should be paying attention to, he does not. The person who he should be ignoring, he gives all his undivided attention to.

In time, you may know. As of right now, you have other concerns. Why I was not able to rear you like I wanted to is not important now. Know that I was and still am with you every step of your living and in your dying.

"So you know everything about me?" Cidal asks.

He does not get a response. He looks at her, waiting for her to speak, but she does not. With a blink of an eye, she is gone.

All Dr. Madglove can do is observe, the tip of the writing utensil presses against the notepad, ready to scratch out any new evidence of his patient's off-centered behavior. Cidal realizes what he has been doing. His eyes shift to meet Dr. Madglove's piercing black pupils blazing like burning coal, studying him, analyzing him, watching his every movement, trying to read his brain that is made of lettuce.

"Pay me no attention," Cidal says. "I lost my head for a minute."

"Do you usually lose your head in the midst of voices?" Dr. Madglove asks.

"What do you mean?"

"Voices seeping in and out of your head. Does this happen often?"

"No, of course not. Voices come from outside, not inside."

"Incredible!" Dr. Madglove scribbles away.

"There's nothing wrong with me, doctor. I can see both sides. That's what I'm told. The breathing world and the non-breathing world. Because…"

"Who told you that?" Dr. Madglove interrupts.

"Mmm…oh! Never mind. You wouldn't believe me."

"I'm a doctor. Try me."

Cidal does not want to go down this particular road. This path leads to the admittance of seeing spirits. He makes a slight left steer to head in another direction.

"My nights, my days are blurred lines. My dreams from my reality walk on the same path. I can't tell which is which anymore. I start off with a certain painting in my head. I paint. But what I have in mind ends up being something totally different. I live. Living seems so real until I wake up to realize I was only dreaming. What I think my reality is…is not really my reality. I'm dreaming. My dreams and reality becomes one big mixture that I can't tell apart. Am I living or am I dreaming? Are you part of my reality or just my illusion?"

Dr. Madglove stares at him as though he was just that. A bizarre character figure of Cidal's wildest imagination. But Cidal is not moved by the oddity of the doctor's mood. He allows him to be. Whatever that is, he lets him be it.

"Which do you think I am?" Dr. Madglove asks. "Real or an illusion?"

Cidal looks at him as he himself appears to be waiting for an answer, and not the other way around.

9

'I don't know why, but she's got something I can't explain,' Cidal says to himself, riding his motor scooter through town.

He arrives back home. As he parks his motor bike in a space provided, he takes one step and sees Ms. Pearly standing at the entrance of the apartment building. He walks slowly towards her.

"Got my money!" she demands more than she asks.

He does not say anything. He only reaches inside his pocket to take out a bank envelope which contains dollar bills. He counts out what he owes silently and gives Ms. Pearly her share. She looks it over. Recounts it to make sure it is exact, then folds and slips it in her upper front pocket of her blouse.

"Didn't think you were gonna pay."

"I said I was."

"That don't mean nothing. You said lots of things that never come true."

"But that doesn't mean I don't want them to come true. They just don't sometimes. That's all. I would never cheat you out of your money. Sometimes I need some time."

"You working? You got paintings all over that apartment. With your job and all that clutter up there, you should be able to make timely payments. Sell some of that junk that nobody wants. Then you'll be able to have something to tie you over. And stay off those substances whatever they are."

She leaves him before he can say anything.

'I'm glad,' Cidal says under his breath. 'It saves me from being rude and walking away from her.'

Out comes his mobile phone after kicking his shoes off and plopping on the couch. A WeChat message he sends to Wei Mei. Instead of waiting for a response, he washes up and goes to his easel. Sitting. Staring. Trying to figure out how best to bring images from escaping his mind to physical reality. The trouble is that he has to stop himself for thinking too much about his art instead of allowing his spirit to create it. This is the key to unlocking what is on the inside and to bring it to the outer world.

He is a visionary who lives in a world where mind thoughts dominate. The mind is led by sight and sound, touch and smell. The spirit is led by none other than itself. The mind follows the senses. The spirit takes lead of the senses. To find his spirit, Cidal knows he has to lose his mind.

His interruption is a WeChat message from Wei Mei:

I miss you. Come visit.

He gathers himself to make a journey to the hotel on his motor bike. He parks in the lot provided for bike vehicles and sends her a WeChat text message. He wants to be certain she is free. Also, making sure that she occupies the same room as before. Room 128.

The door is slightly ajar. So a light touch of a knock is all it takes for her to greet him. Cidal prefers this way of entry. He feels uncomfortable standing, knocking, by drawing attention to himself for those who may be around. Wei Mei's anticipation is spot on within seconds of his soft knuckle brush on the door.

"Ni hao," he says.

"Ni hao," she returns his greeting, quickly closing the door behind him.

The embrace is warm and inviting. Sweet and sensuous. The kiss of their lips meets with a tingle. No small talk. There is no second guessing of what the intentions are. Cidal does not want to be viewed as a cheapskate, wanting a free ride because of her pleasant behavior towards him. His thoughts are: she's only doing her job. He is no more or less desirable to her than any other client. Special attention; extra treatment of how she converses with him. Again, she's only doing her job. Cidal keeps his thoughts on a realistic level. He is not even going to pretend she is all that into him.

"Good to see you," she says, leading him further into the room.

"It's good to see you, too. Can you break away?"

"Break away? I don't know. What you mean?"

"Oh! Can you leave for more than one hour?"

"Leave? Boss no like."

"Does your boss have to know?"

"No make money. Boss very angry."

"I want to take you to dinner."

"Ohhh…"

"So, how's about it?"

"Boss no like."

"Do you want to go?"

"Yes. I like to go."

"Can you ask your boss?"

"No, boss no like. No make money."

"I see. What about later?"

"Later…maybe…okay."

"But you're not sure."

"You come back? Maybe later?"

"I'll be good and hungry before then."

"I no dinner yet."

"Oh? You haven't eaten?"

"No. But maybe I go."

"You will?"

"I make phone call."

Wei Mei hops on her mobile, pushes one button, her call connects. She speaks in Chinese, and as she talks, Cidal sits at the foot of the bed. After one minute or more, she disconnects and slowly lowers the phone down to her side. Her stare into Cidal's eyes is intense, and yet she shows transparency through her pupils. He knows there will be words coming from her eventually, so he holds her captive, floating in the midst of his own irises.

"What you know?" she asks.

"All I know is the Golden Bowl is calling us to come," he replies.

"Is far?"

"Hop on my motor bike. We'll be there before you know it."

Her eyes are locked warmly…tender is her glare. Finally, she says:

"I can't."

"You can't?"

"No, I can't."

"You can change that."

"Yes? How?"

"By saying, you can."

"I can't, but I go."

"Then let's go."

"One hour."

"I promise."

"I hungry."

"So am I."

10

Pulling into the parking lot of the Golden Bowl restaurant on his motor bike, Cidal allows Wei Mei to wear his helmet since he only has one. In spite of the skirt she is wearing, she does not sit side straddle. Once they come to a complete stop, she gets off first, quickly adjusting her skirt so not to show more than she has already shown. Even being in the business that she is in, she still wants to exercise modesty.

A married couple in their fifties owns the restaurant. The wife knows a bit more English than her husband. Wei Mei seizes on the opportunity to speak Chinese to her while ordering.

As they go to a table and sit, she makes a comment.

"Very nice place," Wei Mei says.

"Every time I'm in the mood for Chinese food I come here," Cidal says.

"Often come?"

"Not too often. But often enough."

"I'm glad you like."

Those lingering thoughts of misplacing days, not knowing where those days went still stifles Cidal's mind.

"Did we meet two or three days ago?" he asks.

"Two or three days? I don't understand."

"I was in your hotel room…"

"Yes. We meet first time."

"No. I remember that. But did we meet again late at night?"

"No, we no meet."

"I was in your room. I wanted to see you. After your working hours when there were no clients. We laid on your bed and talked. I rolled off and landed on the floor. Don't you remember?"

"No. It no happen. Maybe you see another girl."

"No, Wei Mei, it was you. I have no interest in seeing another girl."

"It was no me."

"You sure?"

She can only give him a long stare as though all of his marbles have suddenly run out of his pocket.

"What are you thinking?" he asks.

"You, I think. You no feel well. You need Chinese Traditional Medicine to make better."

"Is that right? What do you suggest?"

"Suggest?"

"Yeah. What would you say?"

"Maybe acupuncture. Maybe massage."

"If you are performing it, how much will it cost me?"

Plates, small bowls of different Chinese dishes are brought to the table by the woman co-owner. She lays everything out.

"Enjoy," she says with a smile, "I hope you like."

Wei Mei responds in Chinese to her before she leaves the table. Then, her focus continues on the question that was asked.

"Why you ask me cost?"

"Everything has a price tag on it."

"Oh! Even me."

"I asked you out, so I'm willing to pay for dinner. Will this cost me more?"

"I don't understand."

"Am I also paying for my time spent with you?"

Wei Mei does not answer right away. She points out what food is on which plate, which bowl. Chopsticks are used as she directs, names, and picks up items of food for him to try. The satisfying taste of each delicacy, sips of a small cup of tea. When Cidal is preoccupied with what is in front of him, she redirects the course back to his question.

"You pay to spend time with me, I would say. I no say."

Cidal stops.

"So, I'm not being charged for the hour of your companionship?"

"I have told."

"You told what?"

"I no say."

"Oh, I get it. If you were going to charge me, you would've said. But you didn't say."

"That's right."

"Thanks. Maybe."

"Why maybe? You don't spend money. You save."

"Okay."

"Why you no get married?"

"I would like to one day."

"45 years. No marry? Why?"

"I was trying to get ahead. Never met the right one. Maybe I wouldn't be a good husband. Maybe women see this in me."

"See you no good husband? Why?"

"They see I'm not good husband material."

"Why they see?"

"Can't support nobody with a maintenance job and paintings that don't catch anybody's eye."

"Your painting will catch eye of somebody."

"Yeah. When I'm probably dead. You know how that goes."

"No, I don't know."

"An artist can struggle to create their work. Can't sell it. No interest from nobody. The artist dies. Everybody comes out of nowhere, comes out from everywhere to buy up every piece of art that artist created. Why not buy when life is still circulating? Not just for me. But for any artist."

"About this, you feel strong."

"Naw…I'm just beefing off. Art has more meaning when it struggles to get recognition. When it makes money…too much money, it loses its appeal. It becomes too ordinary. Nothing special."

"I want to see."

"See what?"

"Your painting."

"I want to paint…"

"You paint what?"

"Paint you."

"Ahhh…but I'm not beautiful."

"You don't think so?"

"No like other woman."

"Your naturalness and mystery is more beautiful."

A strange dial tone comes from her purse. She looks to see the caller.

"I know," Cidal says. "I know who it is."

"You right," she says. "Boss."

She slips her phone back inside her purse. "What boss want, I see later."

"Did you call your boss before we left?"

"No. I call Xia cover for me."

"Xia?"

"Girl I work with. She is friend, too."

"Will you get married one day?"

"I don't know. Maybe. I'm 30. Chinese man like young girl."

"30 years old is still young."

"Not for woman in China. Most woman marry before 30. Career woman after 30. Her chance to marry is zero. Man is lucky. He can marry older."

"I see your point. Like me at 45."

She only laughs.

"Well, I'm sure you'll get married. Does it bother you?"

"No. Mother bothers about it."

"Oh…she wants you to get married."

"She thinks no man want to marry me. Me 30."

"I see. Do you have a boyfriend back in China?"

"Hmm…"

Wei Mei does not reveal either way if she has one or not. Cidal is left to guess. However, he refuses to play guessing games.

He is beyond the years of foolish, young folk's charades. Steady. Solid. As much as he can be. He dismisses any notion of trying to figure out what makes her tick. He decides to let her be who she is…whatever she is…whatever she wants to be. To him, it does not matter.

"Either way, you'll find someone," he says, shrugging his shoulders as though he could care less if she reveals to him what her boyfriend status is. "Everybody doesn't always need someone."

"You need someone?"

"Oh, so you're asking if I have a girlfriend. I see how it goes. Like you said, 'Hmm.'"

Unsurprisingly, she gives him a half smile without comment.

Surprisingly, without expectation, Blue Beans makes his way into the restaurant, looks around, spots Cidal, and sits at a table not too far from them. Cidal notices him right away. Their eyes take hold of each other. Blue Beans still carries a crazed look inside his glare. Wei Mei looks in the same direction that has Cidal's attention. She looks back to him.

"Why you look?" she asks.

"The guy that just came in," he says.

She turns her head for a glance of two seconds, and then looks back at Cidal…puzzled. She shakes her head. "I don't see."

Blue Beans appears to know how their conversation is going. He gives Cidal a wink and an okay sign with his hand to signify that this is between Cidal and him. No one else is included.

11

The weekend is long and uneventful. Especially, for someone who lacks activity of moving about. He wants to see and do more than he can. Resources hinder him from obtaining what he really desires. He is trapped inside this world, this society that demands much of what the human male species should accomplish. Anything less than that is unacceptable.

He is not there yet. Most likely, he will never reach his ultimate purpose of what is expected. His passion is to do what burns from within. Paint. Create. To touch into the realm of the unknown by bringing art to it.

He is not in the spring. Nor is he in the summertime. His steps are in line, heading into, or nearly into his season of autumn. These should be years of enjoyment. No longer ignorantly young, living invincibly. But not yet feeling the crisp chilly wave of winter's uncaring hand. At first he is reluctant. However, now he accepts where he is in life. Half of his life or slightly more than half has been completed. 45 years of age is half of 90. Chances of reaching the ninth decade is very slim for him. Why? Because this goal is not worth attaining. His milestone will be at 55 if he is lucky.

He has no fear of death; therefore, he is not afraid to live. Living is his agony. Death can only bring him his reward.

Knowing this, feeling this, he goes out and makes the most or less of his existence. If he dies today, or on some faraway tomorrow, what difference will it make? He walks a thin line, split down the middle. One natural. One spiritual. Mind versus soul. Or both working interchangeably. He has not figured out which. So his battles continue.

12

Bored with himself, tiresome of his creative mode of painting, he escapes out of his apartment and into the streets of Rising Falls. The circulation of people; autos and motor scooters beeping horns; talking, sitting, walking, gathering is the usual popular activity on a Saturday mid-afternoon. A rumbling stomach causes him to stop at a small open door restaurant once again where uncle seems to always be sitting in front of.

"Hi, uncle," Cidal says.

"Hey, sonny," he responds back. "Hungry, huh? They'll serve you inside."

"Thanks."

Cidal goes in to give his order at the counter, and then takes a seat at a table. He is three-quarters finished with his meal when uncle comes strolling in to provide company.

"You got any good word?" uncle asks.

"No," Cidal says. "Just the fact my boss thinks I'm crazy. She may be right. I'm losing sight of where I should be or where I think I'm at."

"Maybe your boss is the one who is crazy."

"She made me see this Dr. Madglove. Some psychiatrist. If not, my job would've been lost."

"To be normal is not to be human. We all are abnormal. Some more than others. That's the way I see it."

"I see your point. I never thought of it that way."

"The ones who think other folk is crazy, is the craziest of all. And that doctor…Madglove…he shouldn't even be practicing. And that's exactly what he's doing. Just practicing. He ain't no real doctor, if you ask me."

"You know him?"

"Heard of him? Who hasn't? He needs his head examined for examining other folks. A crackpot is what he is."

"You don't hold back, do you?"

"If you lived as long as I have, nothing really matters anymore. Or everything matters if one chooses to look at it that way. Either way, you get the same results. A bunch of nothing."

"You seem to be healthy for your wiser years. How do you maintain?"

"I eat whatever I want in moderation. Drink in moderation. Never exercised a day in my life. And mostly importantly, I stay away from doctors."

Cidal laughs. "Stay away from doctors? Why?"

"Don't you ever read the newspapers? Listen to the news? As much of a developed nation that they say we are, we're the sickest people on earth. Third world folk is more healthy than we are. And you know why?"

"No, why?"

"Because of doctors. Doctors and medicine is making us sicker than dogs. And the government is helping them out too. Them low down dirty snakes in grasses. They inject all of these generic modified organisms in our food to make it last longer or make them bigger. Not just our meats, but the fruits and vegetables too. We walking around inflicted with cancer, diabetes, high-blood pressure, and who knows what else. Some sickness they haven't even thought up yet, we'll soon to get it. You can go to the doctor perfectly health. Then, they try to say, *oh you got this or you got that. We need to examine further. You need medication. We need to operate.* Next thing you know, you laying up in some hospital bed with all kind of tubes coming outta you. And ain't nothing wrong with you in the first place. They making us sick and taking our money. And they know it. Medical practice has become a big business. They no more concern about our health than slimy rats. Lab rats! That's what we are to them. Nothing but Guinea pigs."

"I see your point, uncle."

"Sure you do. It's common sense. This so-called richest country on earth has the poorest health of anybody on earth. Years ago, doctors used to care about the health of people. They don't anymore. They care more about dollars. The sicker you are, the happier they are, the richer they are."

"You're so right, sir."

"Of course I am. Is what you do to prevent from getting sick, then you won't have to see them. Unless you're in an accident or something."

"I'll have to remember that. The food is always delicious. Thanks."

"You're welcome, young man."

Cidal finishes the last speck of his food. Uncle sits and observes. It dawns on him.

"Never did get your name."

"Oh, it's Cidal."

"Cidal?"

"Yes."

"Ever think about changing it?"

"Maybe. But it suits me. What's your name, sir?"

"Ease. As in easy does it."

"Glad to know you, Uncle Ease."

"You ain't married, I know. Gotta girl? You seeing someone?"

"Gotta girl, no. Maybe I'm seeing someone. Only in flashes."

"Hmm. Come and go, huh?"

"She's an escort from China. She's here only for a small amount of time."

"Is that so?"

"You think that's bad?"

"Naw…I ain't said nothing. If it works for you, go ahead and do it."

"I can't see her that often. It takes money. I'm poor, a working man who also paints. Have you ever paid for an escort?"

"Naw…can't say that I have."

"You think I'm foolish for doing it, though, huh?"

"I'll tell you one thing, sonny. We men have needs. Women can fulfill those needs. And they know this, too. They have what we men all desire. And they have all the will and power to do what they want to with it. Some men hire escorts. Some men have wives. Some men have both. An escort to help relief the stress built up by the wife. No matter which category of man you fall under, the bottom line is you're still paying for it. One woman is supposed to be more respectable while the other woman is not. Hogwash! There's no difference. With escorts, you pay by your wallet. With wives, you pay through the nose."

13

Cidal walks down the streets of the city. No particular place to go. Killing time; expending energy; collecting thoughts. His artwork is foremost on his mind. It enlivens his soul. His spirit needs to expand. Voices in his head want him to constrict. Polar opposites pulling him, stretching him in contrary directions. He mumbles as he strolls.

'Art is so expressive. Art is so subtle. All at the same time. My next painting has to jump out and still be silent.'

He sits and observes people. He imagines himself as one of them, and then another, wondering what their story is, putting him inside their bodies, their minds to see how they would view the life around them. This way he can eliminate himself to be someone else in order to usher in a different perspective for creative purposes. He is not wishing to be them. His only concern is within himself. He is tired. He is bored of himself. He cannot get out of his own way for his own escape.

Blue Beans stands across the street…motionless. Cidal does not see him right away, but eventually their eyes meet. People and traffic move between them. Everything slowly becomes blurry to Cidal, but the motions are still at a normal pace. When he thinks darkness will encompass his sight, slowly everything becomes as it was before. He expects Blue Beans to be gone, to disappear into thin air, but he remains, still staring with half-crazed eyes.

'Man, that dude gets around,' Cidal says to himself. 'I can't figure out who he is or what he wants.'

Blue Beans makes his move. Gradually, he walks across the street in heavy traffic with fixed, unblinking eyes targeting Cidal. In his awkward stroll, his legs churn as though he is pedaling a bicycle. Safety is of no concern to him. Drivers blast their horns, vehicles slam brakes, voices scream out their frustration towards someone who does not seem to care if his life is put in jeopardy. He makes it across without a touch of danger on his skin. He stands directly in front of Cidal.

"You don't mind if I plop down next to you?" Blue Beans asks.

"You took a big chance coming across the street like that," Cidal says.

"It ain't no mind, it ain't no mind." He takes his seat next to Cidal. "Beautiful day, ain't it? All days here in Rising Falls is beautiful, wouldn't you say? Don't talk much, don't you?"

"No, I guess not. You could've gotten yourself killed."

Blue Beans laughs. "Ain't this somethin'? Look who's talking about killing theyself. You got your nerve, brother."

"You don't know anything about that. You're talking crazy."

"You're in denial. I knows it all."

"I still can't figure out how you know me."

"You ain't gotta figure out nothing. This ain't no math. You just know or you don't know."

"I guess I don't know."

"You can say that again. That's for sho."

"You get around. I see you everywhere now."

"And I sees you motor scootin' that gal."

"When?"

"Restaurant!" Blue Beans says, slightly annoyed.

"Oh, yeah. We saw each other there. You have no trouble finding me. What do you want?"

"Nothin'. Why should I want?"

"You must want something from me."

"I ain't got nothin' on you, Suicidal. I mean Cidal. Same thang."

"You know way too much about me. What gives?"

"Nothin' gives, cause nothin' ain't taken."

Cidal is not even close to being perturbed about this strange occurrence. Likewise, Blue Beans is not trying to be superficial with him either. He is not trying to upstage Cidal with obscure dramatics. He is who he is. So is Cidal.

"You called me Suicidal at first. Why? My name is Cidal."

"Same difference. You is natural in that."

"Natural in what?"

"Killing yourself. Ain't nothin' wrong with it. You're in a recycle stage."

"Recycle stage? What are you talking about?"

"Life depends on death in order for death to recycle back into life. We all have been there. Welcome back. Or welcome forward. It's all the same."

"You talk crazy on one side of your mouth. Then wise on the other side. Which one are you? Crazy or wise?"

"That's up to you. If you ask me, I is crazy. Just like you is."

"You must be some kinda spirit or something. Like Mother…" Cidal stops.

"Mother who?"

"Never mind."

"You think I'm some kinda spook?" Blue Beans laughs. "Then if I is, everybody in town can see me. Why else would they stop traffic for my passing?" He laughs again. "You is crazy! I can see that right now."

"Then how do you know me?"

"From way back. I says before…from way back. You ain't changed none. Still look the same way and all."

Nothing more is said. They sit and observe their environment. Minutes go by. Cidal really wants to be alone to gather his thoughts. He does not need Blue Beans to be his distraction. It would be rude to get up and walk away to find another location where he can enjoy solitary moments. So he sits hoping Blue Beans would eventually be on his way. However, Blue Beans senses this vibe pouring out of every pore of Cidal. He sits with no intention of ever making the first move of departure. There is only one way of ensuring this. Loose conversation.

"I likes it here," Blue Beans says. "Here in Rising Falls. It ain't no other place I wanna be. It gots everything I want. Everything I don't want, it gots that too. You know what I mean."

"No, I don't," Cidal says.

"Course you do. You bright enough. I knows you knows. Don't try to pretend."

"Okay, I know." Cidal says this without having any idea what Blue Beans is leading him into.

"You don't knows. You just saying you knows to shut me up. Well, I ain't about to neither. And there ain't no way you can escape me. Try as you may…"

Cidal's soul becomes a cushion pad for penetrating needles. Without exploding into a cry of anguish, he gradually stands up and quietly walks away.

Further away from where he started, his pace quickens. In spite of his surrounding, he picks up a standing or walking audience while he breezes through the streets with deranged thoughts coming out as conversation to himself.

'Rarely involved with anything
but easy to believe in something
connected to everything
but attached to nothing
my belief is no more correct than anyone else's
their belief is no more correct than mine
arguing, bickering, guessing
will continue 'til the end of time
other galaxies exist
to think that we are alone
mind is stoned as dry bones
a turning point in the course of events
life is like a watershed

hearing birds chirruping
wishing I was dead
the more intelligent you seem
the more dumb you are
the more dumb you seem
the more intelligent you are
it's not what you know
it's what you don't know
so go ahead and be as bright as the sun
and highly evolve yourself into oblivion
mother earth has yet to lose her worth
in a few hundred years
she will be crying tears
a black sun is no good for the universe
and all the births that's in your purse
where do babies come from?
they come from the sky
the day I die
being able to fly
flying right up into…
I don't know
if we take all the weapons that kill
and transform them naturally into weapons that heal
we would all live to be a thousand
it's easy to see
in everyone's life
they need me
so do not weep

when I come to creep
and lay my head to sleep
with nature and spirit there is free will
with man there is nil
with feet planted on the ground
reaching up to touch a cloud
going to sleep each night
hoping to wake up
waking up each morning
wishing to go back to sleep
a strong wind blows me into outer space
no longer wanting to be part of the human race
after I die
going back to whatever I did
before I lived
for this to my life I give
lonely but happy
not lonely but unhappy
if our Creator had a problem with nudity
we would all be born without a booty
stick to whatever works for you
if it doesn't work
do that too
a new day is coming
and if…
well
every day is a new day
every rear end needs to be slapped

shhhhhh!

it's time for me to take a nap.'

Cidal stops his roll to catch his balance. He goes into a stage of hallucination. The bright golden sun becomes black. He collapses.

He hears a voice. He slowly opens his eyes to see he is in the recliner of Dr. Madglove's office. He looks around dazed. He wonders how he got there. The doctor is sitting across from him fiercely taking notes on his pad. He realizes that Cidal has stopped. He pauses his writing and studies him, waiting to hear what else he has to say.

"Is there more you need to add?" Dr. Madglove asks.

Cidal lays his head back against the chair. His words have lost its tongue.

<h1 style="text-align:center">14</h1>

Some female companionship. Someone to talk to, to connect with. A womanly nature to soothe and enhance rather than being bothersome; a burden of agitation. In Cidal's mind, is there such a woman that exists? Maybe.

Wei Mei is sitting still for a pose. Cidal sketches her on his easel in his apartment. He presses with impressions of his artwork. He does not want to portrait her as she is, but his artistic desire is to create her mystery of who she is or who she is not. To keep the viewers of his art piece analyzing, guessing, coming up with their conclusions about her definition. Only her eyes will give away her ethnicity; never skin-tone, nor race. Her implicit elements will speak rather than her explicit nature.

"You paint me. I don't understand." She is puzzled. "There is girl more charming."

"It isn't your physical looks I'm after. It's deeper than your facial expressions or what's on the surface."

"What you say? I don't understand."

Cidal walks over to her. He orchestras his hands over her face down to her body. "I don't want this." He points his finger against her chest. "I want what's inside here. It's your soul, not your body I'm after."

"You have drawing of me?"

"I'm only doing sketches to capture your aura. No paint. That will come later."

The bright natural lighting of early morning filters the room. Cidal keeps an eye on the clock. He does not want to extend her time longer as he desires. Many more minutes elapses before he is through.

"There. I think I captured what I'm searching for. What time do you need to be back at the hotel?"

Wei Mei glances at her watch. "Half past eight."

"It's around 8:00 now. I better take you back. I don't want your boss to throw a fit."

She giggles, but only slightly. "You will finish when?"

"I don't know. My head is swimming with many art pieces. I'm still trying to find that idea."

"Oh? I don't give you idea?"

"Yes, you do. It takes time. I'll let you know when."

"I go before?"

"You go before?"

"Yes."

"You go before what?"

"Leave Rising Falls."

"Oh! When do you leave?"

"I don't know. Now any day. Maybe. What boss say, I do."

"Touch me."

"Why touch you?"

"I just want you to."

She does more than that. She embraces him tightly. "You like?"

"Yes, I like. I wanted to be sure I'm not having one of those spells."

"Spells?"

"Yeah. Not knowing if I'm coming or going." He checks his watch. "We gotta get going."

As they climb on the motor scooter, Ms. Pearly's apartment is on the ground floor in front. She sits inside by the window with curtains barely open to conveniently get every peek of the comings and goings. Her eyes pierce its stare in their direction. Cidal revs up the motor, Wei Mei hangs on tight wearing his helmet. They swiftly leave the premises.

Arriving at the hotel parking lot, he parks in the same place as before. He turns off the motor bike. She takes off the helmet and climbs off first.

"I will go," she says.

"I will walk you up to your room."

"No. I go alone. Boss may be there."

"Okay. WeChat me once you're inside your room."

"Okay."

He watches her stroll away until she is out of view, until she is inside of the hotel. He gets off his scooter and loiters around close by, keeping his eye on the hotel entrance. Expectation is that she will not contact him immediately. He allows her time to get her bearings; to settle back into her routine before her call of clients start to roll in. However, he guesses only to be several minutes, maybe 15 to 20 minutes at best. A half-hour goes by, and then 45 minutes. He sends a WeChat message to her. It falls on deaf ears. One hour slips by. This is his signal to quietly say good-bye.

Cidal arrives back at the parking lot of his apartment. He can see from a distance, Ms. Pearly sitting outside of the building in a patio chair with an expression of wanting to start something. He can feel her bark within himself before she has a chance to open her mouth. He parks his motor scooter and approaches the building. Her viper glare shouts, but her voice is quiet. She speaks when he is a few feet away.

"I see what you're doing. Shagging up with that gal."

"No, I'm alone, Ms. Pearly. You're imagining things."

"I ain't imagining nothing. I saw you when y'all left here. You shagging up with that gal overnight."

"No, you're wrong. I went to pick her up early this morning. I just took her back now."

"I didn't see you bring her here. I don't miss nothing. You snuck her in here late last night."

"I didn't, but the next time I may do that."

"You oughta be shamed yourself. Fornicating on the Lord's Day."

"We did no such thing. I'm painting her."

"Yeah, I bet. Stark naked."

"No. It's respectful."

"She ain't from around here. Where's her folks?"

"Back in China, I guess. How come you're not in church?"

"I only go about two Sundays out of every month. That's all I need. I was going today, but I had to keep my eye on you."

"Don't worry yourself about me. I'm 45. I can keep an eye on myself." Cidal glances at his watch: "You still got time to make the 11:00 service. I'll see you when you get back." He goes up to his apartment.

Ms. Pearly sits in aggravation.

'Lowdown, dirty dog,' she says to herself. 'Instead of sleuth-footing with that gal, he needs to get a real job. Ain't no way she wants him. She'll soon find out. Once she does, she'll be crying onion juice. Let me get up from here and go see what this preacher saying.' She rises and goes back inside to get ready for services.

His shoes shuffle across the floor, pacing back and forth, occasionally taking glances of his sketches of Wei Mei. He checks to see if she has sent a WeChat message. She has not. He initiates contact by sending her a message.

Waited for your message. Didn't get. Everything fine?

A voice comes out of thin air. *She will not answer.*

He turns in a startled panic and sees Mother Goddess materializing, sitting on the sofa, filing her nails. Not once does she look at Cidal.

"Oh! How do you know?"

She has more important business to attend to.

"She could at least let me know that she got to her room without any problem."

Yes, she could have but didn't. What will you do about it?

"What should I do? I'm sure she's got clients now. So I won't bother her. I just wanted to let her know I waited for her message."

Yes...I heard.

"You don't seem to be interested one way or another."

Maybe I know how everything will turn out. These are just preliminaries for a future showdown.

"Would you care to enlighten me?"

Humans are amazing. You all want to know what's ahead in your life. You should enjoy the ride that is provided and not be overly concerned about what's around the corner or further over the horizon. If you knew, you would never live your life to the fullest potential. Not knowing is more alluring. Discovery is everything. Explore.

"If that's how it will be, then why should I care?"

You're learning. Besides, why should a dead man be concerned about living?

For the first time since appearing, she looks at him. Cidal stares back at her.

"What do you mean by that?" he asks.

Taking your own life. If you're bold enough to die, why not be bold enough to live? And if your living is bold enough, it may eventually lead to your death.

"Which side are you on? The side of life or the side of death?"

Death is life revitalized. One really has not lived until one dies. The soul's unlimited potential can only happen in death. You cannot have one without the other. You are living prove.

"But I am alive."

Your line of life and death is very thin. Converging onto each other. She goes back to filing her nails.

"So what should I do about Wei Mei?"

Do whatever you want to do. Still filing her nails without the least concern about Cidal's plight. *It really does not matter. You will end up having the same fate. Asking questions does not sound like you. Why should you care?*

"Getting with this girl could prolong my life here on earth. There will be something to live for."

What if she is not what you thought she would be? Then, you would be back to square one. You would want to die even more.

"I would never give any woman that satisfaction. For her to think that I'm so heartbroken over her that I would take my own life. I can do that much all by myself without pitying myself over some woman."

Yes, and you have done magnificently diluting in your own misfortunes.

"Not only that, I hardly know her."

It is always what you do not know that holds your heart hostage.

"What do you mean?"

Unknown elements drive us over the edge of a cliff; sinks us through the hole of the universe. Madness comes when one cannot figure things out. A man learning to cope with female intuition is no different. Strength is in subtleties, not in might.

She says all of this without one direct look at Cidal. Filing her nails; philosophical jargon as though it is second nature. She is of the spirit world, so this is nothing out of the ordinary for her.

His ability to see and hear her is never too much concern. Others may have been tossed to higher skies, drifting on a cloud because of experiences with an entity not of this world. Cidal refuses to be yanked into a feeling of specialty. His footing securely follows natural ground.

"So what is your purpose of showing up?" he asks. "There must be some message you need to give to me. Something I have to receive from you."

Once again, you are on a balancing beam of life and death. You can smell the aroma. You can taste the spices of both sides and see how you like it. The meal has been prepared for you. Instead of turning up your nose of what is provided, indulge in the savor of every flavor.

A knock on his door grabs his attention. He goes to answer it. Ms. Pearly stands before him in her Sunday's best.

"Who's in there with you?" she asks. She tries to look around him to see for herself.

"Nobody," he says. "Just me."

She lightly brushes her arm against him to enter the room. She glances around. Mother Goddess holds her positon without interruption, still filing her nails. It is obvious to Cidal that Ms. Pearly cannot see her.

"You must be talking to yourself, then," Ms. Pearly says.

"I do that lots of times. Whose voice did you hear?"

"Yours of course. You talking like you in conversation with somebody but ain't nobody sayin' nothin' but you. I knew you were crazy."

"Well, I don't want you to be late for services."

"You need to go yourself. Maybe the pastor can pray that slothful, uncaring spirit outta you."

This is why I never attended church services when I was alive. Mother Goddess chimes in without one glance.

"Me and church don't agree," Cidal says to Ms. Pearly, trying to ignore what was said by his unseen guest.

"And that's exactly your problem. You don't agree to nothin' but a whole bunch of foolishness. I'm gone. I'm already late."

Ms. Pearly breezes out as quickly as she breezed in. The door is fastened.

It has been my experience that those who are the most religious on earth are the least spiritual in the spirit world. Those who are the least religious on earth are the most spiritual after this life.

"Why is that?" Cidal asks.

Religion forces those to expect certain things after their time is up in this world. Everything they are taught from their religion never comes to pass. Those who do not learn of any teachings of religion are far better off. They do not come into the spirit world with any expectations embedded in their natural minds. They are more open and willing to accept anything and everything.

Cidal stares at her. She will not take one look at him. She does not need to. He can only nod his head in agreement.

15

A bright vision emerges from a gloomy, narrow reflection. Protruding thoughts which keep him up from midnight to sunrise. A peaceful sleep without disturbance. A moonbeam connects with the light in his soul. To gain happiness without force. Lonely depression disappears from course. Pursuing dreams of his heart's desire. To actually see them transpire. A true love that does not belong to someone else. No need for anyone but him. In a twinkling of an eye, having all of his troubles subside. Possessing all the knowledge of this world. Obtaining all the wisdom in the life to come. Comfortable materially; prosperous spiritually in all of its total sums.

For he has not seen nor has he experienced any of these things. To speak of matters which are not visible and willing to see them come to pass. Just to have an insight in what his future may bring. Knowing deep from within that there are such things.

Cidal wrestles with himself, tossing and turning, his mind prevents him from a restful sleep. He refuses to clock watch. He knows it is after midnight, after 12:30, after 12:45, so he gets up and tries his hand at creating art. He scratches out something artistically that he is not completely satisfied with. Always he has been very hard on himself that way. He changes his clothes from pajamas to street, and he heads out into the night.

The streets are quiet at this hour. Hardly any vehicles. Barely any people. Hands are in his pockets, slowly strolling through town. Most stores and shops are closed with the exception of a scattered one or two. A fresh scent is in the air; the temperature is perfect. Pleasantry surrounds. No hint of any malicious behavior lurking about. He finds somewhere to sit.

His mind wanders from thought to thought. His soul aches for a new, a different experience in his art, in his personal life. Sickened by who he is, Cidal has flash images of the various ways to end his life:

Drowning by walking further out into the sea

Self-inflicted gunshot to the brain or abdomen

Jumping off a cliff

Standing in the way of a speeding vehicle

Poison by liquid or capsule

Lying in bed, day-in, day-out, without food or drink

Recklessly behind the handlebars of his motor scooter heading into an abyss

To be shot by a jealous husband, or better yet, be killed by a female lover

History of the "black dog" snapping at his hind.

But the most painless way to end his life would be the best option. Not because he is cowardly. His feelings go out to the ones who would have to clean up the mess after his departure. This makes him empathetic towards others.

'I can't seem to get out of my own way,' he says to himself. 'What use am I to me or everyone else? What's one less person in this world? My paintings will probably never support me. I'll probably never get married. Never have any kids. I started out alone. I will end up alone. Why bring any kids into this life if I'm not here to see them grow? My miserable genes, they would inherit. That I inherited from whomever. I couldn't do that to them. From the many years of bloodline through many generations, it will stop with me. I won't pass it on.'

Wei Mei remains sleepless in her bed. Her eyes are fixed on the ceiling above. A moon beam comes through the window of her room. She reaches for her mobile phone next to her on the nightstand. Directly, she goes into the WeChat app to view what she had missed throughout her time away.

Girlfriends from back home in China sent her messages, photos, and video of their experiences of recent activities or events. Written articles of various thoughts and topics. After scanning through most, she notices a message sent by Cidal. She reads it. She sends a message of reply.

Sorry no send. Also busy.

A dink comes to Cidal's mobile. He pulls out his phone to see a WeChat message from her. He thinks for a moment before deciding what he will do. He lays his phone next to him, leans back and crosses his arms. No big deal.

She is not expecting a return message from him at this late hour. Her mobile is back on her nightstand. Sleep still is a stranger to her. Foreign…her body does not know it. Her mind drifts.

Many cities throughout the country she has been. Several other countries too. If it was not for her trade, she would not have enough resources to venture out of China. Men of western and non-western persuasion have certain fetishes for certain characteristics of women. Being from a culture where women are shrouded in mystery, femininity, and possessors of subtle sensuous allure, she and others bring an ancient womanly appeal to men who yearn for it.

Cidal picks up his phone again and rereads the message. For one second of one moment, he looks away in thought. Then he decides to respond very simply and directly.

Okay

He lays his phone back down beside him. 'I won't get too far in conversation. She'll take her time in responding anyway.'

A slight sound goes off on her mobile. Wei Mei turns to see that she has a WeChat message. Her first thought is from family or girlfriends back in China. From where she is at in America, China is exactly 12 hours ahead in time. Her after midnight hours is synonymous to their afternoon delight. When she realizes who it is from, she immediately sends back a reply.

You wake up?

This time Cidal is surprised to get such a quick response from her. He replies to her:

Yes I am

There is light corresponding between them. Before the main point is taken.

> *Why still up?*
> *Can't sleep*
> *You can't sleep why?*
> *Maybe same reason you can't*
> *My day long*
> *You should be sound asleep then*
> *True this is not*
> *You in bed?*
> *Yes. And you?*
> *No, I'm in the middle of town sitting*
> *Why? Fresh air will you sleep?*
> *I'm on my way. When I knock, you will know who it is*

Wei Mei does not respond because she has no idea of what to say. So she lays there. Still staring at the ceiling. She turns to her side and looks at the glow of the moon's spirit filtering into her room. Her anticipation is uncertain. There is a mystery, an unknowing of what to expect. Minutes of 15 or more passes. Her eyelids are losing to the weight of sleep. In-between the stages of conscious and sub-conscious, right when she thinks she is still awake, but her hand is on doorknob of entering into the depth of dreams, there is the sound of knocking. She lets it go. She is dreaming. The knocking still continues. She realizes that her dreams have been reversed. She opens her eyes and sits up in bed. She swears she has not been asleep. But she has. One knock. Two light knocks.

Climbing out of bed, she pops on the nightstand lamp, and goes to the door. She focuses as she peeks through to see if it is really him. It is. The door opens wide enough for Cidal to slip in. She closes it. No greeting of words. She thinks she already knows what he wants. He can read her mind. He shakes his head indicating negativity. Takes her by the hand and walks her to the bed. He lays her down and turns off the lamp.

"You pay?" she asks. He says nothing.

So sure of what he is doing, he refuses to answer any questions. He kicks off his shoes. From his left knee in front of her on the bed, to his right knee behind her, he straddles to position himself where he lays directly behind to spoon her. He wraps his arm around her body. In her ear, he whispers:

"I know the routine. One pays for time and companionship and not sex. I'm wasting your time for companionship only. Will you charge me?"

She reaches back slightly to touch his cheek. Then, she faces away from him, allowing him to have his moments of closeness. This is not only for him. She needs intimacy as much as he does. Her business requires something other than familiar connections. It takes a lot out of her, any woman of this profession. Her emotions…her psyche are affected with every encounter. Her femininity takes a beating like a punching bag. Her bed, a gym mat for every guy who wants to pay for a workout. But Cidal seems to be different. She senses his sensitivity. This is new. This is welcoming to her.

She is touched. But she is also cautious. Very practical. She has to be. Visiting a country that has a different culture than her own, Wei Mei is prepared to guard herself from intentions of men not familiar to what she is used to back home. She carries herself in ways that is never intimidating or threatening. Her poise attracts attention. She notices this. Not only of her, but other women of her culture.

"You like me?" she asks.

"Yes. I guess I do," he replies.

"You no sure?"

"Maybe I am."

"Why you like? Because I Chinese?"

"Why you ask?"

"Many man like Asian woman…Chinese woman."

"Oh, I see."

"You will not say?"

"Say what?"

"You like because I Chinese."

"No, I will not say."

"Why you no say?"

"It doesn't matter if you are or not."

"You date Chinese woman before?"

"No, I haven't."

"What kind woman you date?"

"No particular kind."

"You have idea woman in mind?"

"I used to. Maybe at one time. Not anymore."

"Why used to? Why not anymore?"

"I've learned my lesson. The idea woman doesn't exist."

"Maybe you are no idea man for woman."

"That's what I came up with. I'm nobody's idea man, so why should I bother any woman."

"Maybe woman wants you to bother her?"

"Believe me. Most don't."

"Maybe change outlook. Maybe can be better."

"Or worse."

"Why you say?"

"It depends on what woman I choose. Each woman has her own temperament…her own mood or behavior. I have enough problems of my own not to inherit more stress. I have to find one who will benefit my life, not destroy it."

"Such woman, no exist."

He laughs. "It took me a long time to realize that."

"You no romantic?"

"Yes, I am. Maybe. It's not for me to say."

"What you mean?"

"It's up to the woman to say that I am. It's not up to me."

"You have low view of you?"

"No, a realistic view."

"Share. I don't understand."

Cidal thinks about what he wants to say. How to say it so she can understand. What he needs to tell her is too involved. Too many words. He breaks it down to simple, something controversial.

"Marriage kills romance. Very seldom does one get both. Very rarely."

Silence overcomes her. Her speech is muted. Cidal feels, he anticipates a minor argument, a major discussion from her perspective, any woman's point of view in favor of a romantic fantasy. He does not try to explain himself to get on her good side. Most men would if they felt they have crossed over to explosive boundaries to save themselves from butting heads, trying their best to avoid unnecessary battles. When he senses she is about to speak, he does not brace himself for a hand grenade to land in the middle of his lap. Really, he could care less.

"I think you right," she says to his surprise. "I see couple married, no romantic. My father, my mother, I don't see love in marriage."

"Yeah? Do they fight?"

"No, fight. Father has duty as husband. Mother has duty as wife. Married more than 30 years."

"They must be doing something right, then."

"But no love. No romance."

"They must like each other to make it work."

"China different than America. Marriage more important in China than here."

"I agree with you. Here, couples divorce because one has cold feet in bed."

Wei Mei giggles at this. "One wear socks to keep marriage working."

"Exactly."

"You prefer?"

"Prefer what?"

"Marriage or romance?"

"I'm too much of a loner to be married. I'm too sensible to be a romantic."

"Ahhh…good answer."

"And you?"

"Hmm. Too sensible to married. Too much loner to be romantic."

"Uh-huh. We seem to be a good fit."

"Maybe."

"Philosophically."

"Oh."

"Shhh…I'm here to make you sleep."

"Yes. Sleep-uh, sleep-uh Cidal baby."

16

No new contract. No new lease. Cidal's life is still as it always been. No bets. Not even one thin dime. His heart refuses to be pulled by any strings. Why? Because he knows his own reality. His destiny is defined. His fate is determined. He is walking inside the footprints of his own choosing or chosen by an entity beyond his control.

Manager Luella keeps watchful eyes on him throughout the working day. She clues in on any behavior that is suspect to insanity. At times, Cidal mumbles to himself. His coworkers are secretively on the lookout for activity that would be sufficient enough for his dismissal. The coworkers become the manager's eyes, her ears when she is not around.

He has been seen to stop in the middle of his duties to have a conversation with someone who is not there. Of course, he hasn't a clue he is being spied on. Usually, the conversations are not long. He is aware of his surroundings in the workplace. Anyone passing by could have questions, wondering about his mental stability. When he most suspects he is alone, his least expectancy comes to a surprise.

"Cidal." He turns around to discover his manager standing directly behind him. "Come to my office." She walks away. He stops whatever he is doing to follow her. Once she has taken her seat behind her desk, Cidal comes in and closes the door. He immediately sits down. He knows this discussion may be longer than he wants it to be.

"Is there a problem about my work?" he asks.

"I've heard you have gone to see Dr. Madglove," she says, totally ignoring his question altogether just to get to her point. "He is fascinated by what he's observed. I have spoken to him. He feels other appointments are necessary."

"Necessary for him or for me?"

"I don't follow."

"It's a waste of time being there. I'm sure he's got more important sessions with people who really need them."

"You don't feel that you need them?"

"To be honest with you, Luella, I don't."

"As I have said before, you are totally in denial about your condition. You need psychological help and you don't even know it. I've been watching you. Others have watched you also. I believe you're harmless. But I can be wrong. It's better to know more about your state of mind before you hurt yourself and possibly others around you. I could never forgive myself if that ever happened. I feel that I'm responsible in some way."

"Do I still have my job if I refuse to keep going?"

Luella pierces him with her eyes. "Why would you stop going? Considering it does you more good than harm."

"Will I still have my job?"

She remains silent. Then she speaks. "You held up your end of the bargain. Yes, you still are employed here. The only thing that can dismiss you now is yourself."

"Meaning?"

"Meaning your attendance and performance. Whatever your condition is, if it affects your responsibilities and duties when it comes to what is expected here, then I may be inclined to let you go. Understood?"

"Yeah. Loud and clear."

"You may go back to work."

Cidal stands up and walks out. Nothing in his expression shows how he receives the encounter with his manager. No co-worker or acquaintance ever befriends him. He is approachable, but rather keeps to himself working or on break. He never tries to strike up conversation. Nor does he inquire to anyone about anything. His time at work is to get through every ticking hour so he can leave. He is there to make dollars enough to avoid drowning in a sea of income deficiency. Still, he wants to believe that his artwork which has not been sufficient will eventually become sufficient enough to support his life.

He captures the essence of himself by himself. Others are barely his inspiration for what he wants to do…for what he longs to become. Satisfaction comes with his own peace of mind which seems to elude him. He knows his potential. He is aware of his limitations. Late afternoon, he pauses as he walks the streets. He leans against a lamppost somewhere in the middle of town and speaks to himself.

'Whatever I do…no matter what I may be fortunate enough to be successful in my art, I will never obtain greatness. I will always strive to improve to perfection in this lifetime. Once I take my last breath, once I feel myself leaving the hollow cavity of this body---then, and only then will I achieve greatness.'

Onlookers dip in as he is speaking, scanning around them, wondering who this half-crack pot is talking to. When they realize he is talking to himself, they quickly move on. They want no part in what could happen once his light switch flips in another direction. For he is never one to give two cents on how others perceive him, Cidal collects himself and continues his journey.

He thinks of Wei Mei in what she may be doing at this moment. It is late afternoon, before dinnertime. His assumption… she is probably engaged with clients. He checks his mobile to see if he has missed any messages from her on WeChat. She is much as a mystery to him as he assumes he is to her. His mind is analytical on more occasions than not. However, he has not tried to figure her out. He carries many plagues within himself without attempting to climb inside someone else's brain to see how it ticks. He refutes to his inner self that he should play any role associated with the chases of romance. Still, there is no response to his initiation of communication with the Chinese women on the website: China Romance Select. An interest on their part may never reach him. He has developed something with Wei Mei, an escort from China, which he has not established with any woman of "more acceptable professions." And there are many possibilities that they will never make themselves available to him. So he is stuck with the ultimate choice. This may be as good as it gets. He has nothing to really live for, but everything to die for.

In his casual stroll through the city, he spots in the distance, the uncle who owns the small restaurant. As usual, he sits outside watching the slow pace of incomers, out goers up and down the sidewalks and vehicles exercise on the streets. Cidal stops by to chat and sits with him.

"Hello, uncle. Uncle Ease, isn't it?"

"You got that right. What do you say, sonny?"

"It may go against your idea, but I'm thinking about getting married."

Uncle looks away. Then he glares back at him. "What on earth for?"

"I have nothing to lose."

"There's gotta be some reason why. Talk to me."

"I've been thinking. Why not?"

"Who is this chick?"

"Someone most men wouldn't marry."

"Oh, I see. That prostitute from…"

"China, yes, sir."

"She ain't pregnant, is she?"

"No."

"What suddenly brought this on?"

"Nothing at all."

"She ain't forcing you, is she?"

"No. She doesn't even know about it yet. I haven't mentioned it to her."

"Well, I advise you not to mention it to her at all. You gotta be crazy to want to do it on your own accord. If she was making you, well, maybe consider it, but I would still be against it."

"I wanted to throw it out to you first."

"Well, you know how I stand. Nothing good can come out of it. Especially for men. Women got all of the advantages. We men got nothing."

"Maybe, sir, there is something we men can get from it."

Surprised, and out of his mind of what he has just heard, Uncle Ease shoots daggers at Cidal from deep within his pupils.

"You got any reasons why?" he asks Cidal. "No! There're no reasons but excuses. Give me one good excuse why?"

"Well, first, to share my life with someone."

"Negative. There's a price to pay by sharing your life with them. One…your peace of mind goes down and your stress level goes up. Signs of an easy, early death. Name another excuse. And don't say regular sex. I already shot that down some time ago. You get less sex being married than you do being single. So don't even mention that. You can have a girlfriend or girlfriends and get all the sex you want."

"Okay, I won't mention sex then. Well, I am getting older."

"Negative again. Being a man, we can get women of any age that is reasonable. I got this buddy of mine who is 70 years old. His girlfriend is 43. He don't look his age and neither does she. Next excuse."

"I won't mention anything about love."

"You better not either. That love thang ain't nothing more than a farce somebody dreamt up. Poets, songwriters, book writers, movie makers, they all got people believing in something that don't exist. Yeah, love for other human beings and thangs. That's all right. But all that romantic stuff is a bunch of phony baloney. You like each other or you don't. You get along or you don't.

Nothing more. Love? Ha! A bunch of foolishness if you ask me."

"I said to her that marriage kills romance."

"Kills romance? It shouldn't be there in the first place. A man should hold his own. He can be nice to her and be considerate. But that's all he should do. Never go the way of emotion. It kills one's manhood. I'm not saying be a jerk to women either. All I'm saying is that a man should hold his own…hold his ground. The so-called helpmate is not always reliable. Hold your own. Next excuse."

"Let's see. I already said: sharing my life with someone; you shot down steady sex; getting older is not worthy of marriage for men; you also shot down the falsehood of love or romance." Shrugging his shoulders, Cidal says, "I have nothing."

"Good! You don't need nothing either. You got yourself. That's good enough."

"Yes, sir. I guess you're right."

"You hungry?"

"I guess I can use a small bite. A sandwich and pop will be okay."

"Go in there and let them fix you something. I'll still be right here."

"Thanks uncle."

From the time it takes to put in his order, sitting and eating, Cidal walks out of the restaurant within 35 minutes of first entering. Uncle Ease is still where he said he would be.

"Is that gonna last you, young man?"

"Yes, it will do. I'll see you next time. And thanks."

"Remember what I said now. You better not come back married. If you do, you better find some other place to eat."

"Really?"

"Just kiddin'. You're welcome back anytime."

"Sounds good. I will be back."

About one block down from uncle's restaurant, Cidal hears whistling coming from behind him. He casually strolls along. He notices it but he does not give it much attention. A happy song that he is sure he has heard before. Unable to place what song it is, without turning around, he slows his pace for the whistler to catch even with him. The whistler seems to be playing the same game, because he slows down as well, not giving into the passing rights to move in front. Suddenly, Cidal stops. The whistler stops even-steven right beside him. Cidal turns his head to see Blue Beans standing there. He pauses whistling.

"You don't like my whistling? Or is it my song? I'll take requests. What would you like to hear?"

"You pop up everywhere, don't you?"

"I can't place what song that is. Can you hum it?"

"Naw, man, I can't." He continues to walk. Blue Beans goes with him. Side-by-side.

"You don't have no good taste in music…that's all," Blue Beans says. "Ain't it?"

"I guess you're right, green bean…"

"Blue Beans, you nincompoop!"

"Oh, yeah. How could I forget?"

"And I gots better taste in music than you do."

"Okay. Only if you say so."

"Where you heading to?"

"Nowhere in particular."

"Still scuffling after that gal, huh?"

"Why are you so concerned? You shouldn't be."

"I gots to know. Just looking out for ya."

"Really. Thanks, but no thanks. I can handle it."

"We'll see if you can. You might not be able to. Because… there's some thangs you don't know."

This prompts Cidal to stop cold in his tracks. "What things? Things like what?"

"I ain't tellin' ya if you don't know. You'll see."

Blue Beans walks on while Cidal stands and watches.

17

Perhaps it is because of his sensitive nature. She flies just beneath his standard. But just barely. She is not his first choice. Considering his current situation, socio-economical and mental, he has no room to make a judgement against his own preference. She may be his only choice. He convinces himself that this is good enough for him.

Good enough? And why not? Other women on the website China Romance Select, there are many potential mates to choose from. Women from varies backgrounds, ages, occupations, and appearances. The ones who meet Cidal's standards do not seem to take an interest in him. He does not force himself to pursue the lesser ones from his preference bar which in fact is quite realistic. He has never initiated contact with the ones who are too young, but the ones who are young enough. Women who have high degree of accomplishments from their careers, he knows to stay away from. Because he is aware of the possibility of them looking down on him for being in his present condition. Which is what? A struggling artist that pushes brooms and cleans toilets to help make his pay.

So he is in a position to consider someone who is not part of any dating website. Someone who he has met happenstance to keep his libido in practice, to keep it active so he will not lose his desire long before his wisdom age starts to set in. Wei Mei comes in as a portrait of painting, eases into his life, only viewing him as any other client. To both advantage points, this is correct. A fondness begins to settle in. Or at least an imitation of it. This may cause emotional problems to a relationship that is supposed to be intimately professional, and yet unemotional, unattached.

After hours of diligent work, his artistry runs out. Exhausted of what he has put into it. The twilight of evening creeps in. It begins to fade in small increments. A call is put out. Cidal escapes to the outdoors of his apartment. He jumps on his motor bike and coasts up the street towards where his mind has been leading him to. He slows and turns into the parking lot of the hotel. He parks and waits for a few moments. He sends a WeChat message to Wei Mei. He waits. And he waits. When 15 minutes has passed, he can see a silhouette of a female figure walking in his direction. The closer she gets… the more he knows she was able to buy some time.

Light shadows reveal her face when she approaches. Her expression is pleasing. It signifies that she is not disturbed by his desire to see her.

"Ni hao," he greets her.

"Ni hao," she replies back.

"You were able to come. I'm glad."

"See me, you happy?"

"Yes."

"I happy to see you."

"Good. Let's walk."

"Hao de."

"Hao de?"

"Yes. Means okay."

"Okay then. Hao de."

They remain on the grounds of the hotel. There are three separate buildings surrounded by plush gardens and two swimming pools located in different parts of the premises. The evening has a certain gentle kiss of hush. Serenity hovers to the embracing arms of safety. A mockingbird sings a song of love anticipation. This is their cue that it could potentially be for them, and not a male bird's attempt to pursue its own course of mating. No conversation starts out. No hitting and missing between words. Sometimes the lack of speech is better than useless communication. They are not afraid of silence. Nature envelops. An inner vibe develops. Feeling each other without the physical touch.

Quiet does not distract, but provides a comfort when talk has not found its tongue. Eventually, something is said.

"What are you thinking?" he asks.

"Nothing," she says. "Enjoying it."

"Enjoying the evening?"

"Yes."

"Anything else?"

"No."

"I see."

They move on with their casual stroll. Then, she realizes what was implied.

"No. I enjoy you."

"Naw…you don't have to say that."

"I do. I want to say."

"Okay."

"I do not lie to you."

"That's good."

"Woman in China is not like western woman."

"You mean in lying?"

"No. Chinese woman no say about feelings."

"Oh!"

"Western woman say about feelings."

"I think I follow you."

"Why?"

"Why what?"

"Why you follow me?"

"No, I mean I understand you."

"Oh, I understand now."

"Yes, I agree. Here in the west, women talk about their feelings of love."

"Yes. Woman no say in China."

"How do men know if women like them in China?"

"You be around Chinese woman to know."

"That's why I asked."

"Chinese woman no say. Chinese woman do."

"Do what?"

"Woman in China act. No speak-uh. No say. We do."

"Yeah. It's opposite here. People say and don't do."

"Here it's different. I don't understand America way."

"Most of us don't understand our way either."

This sends Wei Mei into a short laughter. "You cute."

"You are cute too," Cidal says.

"Really? Why you say?"

"Because it's true. Don't you think you're cute?"

"No. I'm okay."

"Why do you say that?"

"Some customer no think."

"Don't think what? That you're cute?"

"Yes. They no think."

"To each his own, I guess."

"Some customer picky. I open door. They no come in. They walk away."

"Maybe it's not you. On the website ad, it shows model like girls in their early 20s. When clients don't see what they think they are getting, they turn away. It can't be just you. Because you're not bad looking at all."

"Not all do it. Just some. You no walk away. You like me?"

"Yes, I guess I do."

"You keep come to see me. I like."

"Do I bother you?"

"No."

"You are hard to read. Sometimes I don't know."

"I don't know you. I don't know American man."

"We don't know each other completely. True. It's fun to find out."

"You are happy with me?"

Cidal thinks hard with the passing of several seconds. He decides to take his chances. It will not hurt him. And why should he care what the end results will bring?

"Why you no say?" Wei Mei asks because of his silence.

"Yes, I'm happy with you. I'm not always happy with myself."

"What you mean?"

They come to the part of the grounds where two gazebos looking over a swimming pool located behind one of the hotel buildings. Each gazebo has a square glass table and four high back chairs. They sit, adjusting their chairs to view the swimming pool. The lighting is enough for the area to enjoy a coziness without being to creepy for the approaching night.

"You no say," Wei Mei reminds him. "What you mean? You no happy person?"

Cidal does not want to reveal too much about himself. If she is exposed to his real struggles within himself, she would flee in fear. She is comfortable around him. He does not desire to stir up any misgivings. Besides, he figures that she could have her own turmoil in life. Choosing a profession she has chosen makes him believe that she has.

"I guess I am," he says to save face. "Happy."

"Oh."

"What about you?"

"I guess I am." She says this to mimic him. She feels that he is not sure, so she comes back to him with her own uncertainty. "Happy."

"You know what I'm thinking?"

"What?"

"We should hook up."

"Hook up? I don't understand."

"Get together. You and me."

"Relationship? Marry?"

"Whichever one. We should do it."

Wei Mei is flattered. But at the same time, she does not know what to do or which direction to go. She explores all sides to see where he stands.

"I don't know. I have job. I travel. I don't know how to live here. I like China."

"Our two countries…a big difference in the culture. Could you get used to America?"

"I don't know. My whole life China. Why you want to do?"

"We are different, but the same in a lot of ways. It could be interesting. You don't have to say now. Think about it."

"Will you support me? I can't do. I will burden you."

"I'm a pretty simple man."

"I simple woman."

"I will continue to work. Maybe find something else to do. I will always paint and create art. There's nothing else for me."

"I already poor. Why I do job. To make, save money. I no want to do for rest of life. Try to get other job. Can't find work. Don't pay like this job. This why I work business."

"I understand. We all have to do what we have to do. And besides, I'm not in a position to look for a trophy girlfriend or wife. I am who and what I am. I'm no big deal. Women can do so much better than me. I will never promise what I can't deliver. I have no right to ask any woman what I've asked you."

"You pay me one time for job. Your money is low. You afford me to be girlfriend, wife? How you can afford? I will burden you."

"You're right. Maybe I can't. Skip it."

"Skip it?"

"Yeah. Forget it."

"No. You ask me to think. I will think. Maybe it will. I don't know. You say. I will think."

"It doesn't matter either way. I will not care if you didn't."

"We distant in worlds. Distant in culture."

"Yeah, you're right. We're distant, but not disconnected."

18

From pitch black, eyes slowly open to reveal the dawn of early morning break, slipping its way from the grasp of the darken night's grip. Cidal lies on his back in bed. His eyes fix on the ceiling. He turns to see the red light of his digital clock reading at 5:23. Knowing he has more time to linger in his restfulness, thoughts of his previous late evening with Wei Mei comes to mind.

'I can't ask her a thing,' he says aloud. 'I can't mess up this girl's life. She's better off doing what she's doing than to hook up with me. What can I offer her? Nothing!'

He grabs his mobile which is setting on the nightstand. Swiping into the home screen, he goes to the WeChat app, presses to see if any activity has been directed his way. No messages. It is still in the wee hours of morning. Wei Mei must be asleep. She has a long day of clients ahead of her is what he figures. He shoots her a simple text: *Want to see you again. Soon.* He lays his phone back on the nightstand and flips over to his side with his back towards the alarm clock.

Cidal is awake, but not fully rested. He stares. He does not see objects in the room. His focus eliminates them for his main attraction. He zeros in on nothing. His eyes are distant to another world...another existence...something foreign to the world he finds himself in. To get up? Why? His paintings are not selling. A piece of a two-bit cleaning job pays peanuts. He is no more to Wei Mei than any other customer. He has nothing really to get up for. Nothing to truly live for. What he really wants is to go back to sleep and not wake up at all. Not until he is light-years away from earthly realm.

Notions of sleep still remains. Before he knows it, Cidal is caught between the world of dreamland and reality. His consciousness balances midway. He thinks he hears footsteps coming towards him. He refuses to open his eyes, hoping whatever has invaded his room will go away. He feels the weight of a person sitting on his bed. The bed cover is around the middle of his body. Whoever has decided to sit on his bed, took the initiative to bring the sheet of his covers up to his neck for comfort. The touch of someone's hand glides over his face when he forces himself to awaken to see his intruder. In a flash, he shoots up halfway almost in a sitting position. There is no one.

'I didn't think I was asleep,' he says to himself. 'But I guess I was.'

Of course you were asleep. The sound of a woman's voice rings. Slowly, Mother Goddess materializes. She is sitting on the side of his bed.

"Oh!" He can only say.

Must I remind you? You are living in two worlds simultaneously.

"Yeah. A half walking zombie. Most days I feel like one."

A walking zombie as you put it. The half dead part of you is your life on earth. It wants to remain here. While your spirit is constantly, forever alive. It wants, it needs to move on. Death is never how you imagine it to be. That is the nirvana part of your existence. The spirit is never free until it breaks out of the physical mold of your body. Humans talk of being free spirits? Not when you are trapped inside your flesh. Show me a person who claims to be a free spirit in this world. I will tell them in order to become one, you must die. Flesh and bone are really clones.

"I guess this is my philosophical note for today, huh?"

Label it as you want. She gets up and walks to the center of the room, turns and faces him. *You know I speak truth. Your spirit tells you that. You can feel it.*

He says nothing. He looks at her, and then he drops his eyes onto the bed. Indicating, he knows exactly what she is telling him.

Don't get confused. Your natural world is not your reality. The world of dreams is no fantasy. Why do dreams feel more real than life situations? Because all dreams are spiritual. We are all spirits. This earth is just one passing ground of infinity. Only natural beings mourn for their loss. Spirit beings celebrate. So if you want to end your life completely, go ahead and end it. No one here will weep for you. The spirit world rejoices.

"So it's my choice to live or die."

The transition from this life to the next is not all bad.

"I figured that much. Why do you think I tried to end it? Instead of taking up space and air on earth, why not move on is how I see it. I'll be the better for it. Either or. It shouldn't matter to me. I'll never be one of those success stories that people hear about. With all odds against them, someway, somehow they find ways to dig themselves out and find themselves on top. At this point in my life, I don't have any will or desire to fight uphill battles. We all can't be on top. I've learned to accept everything and to expect nothing in return."

Then why breathe half-heartedly? Why breathe at all? What are you waiting for? If you have nothing to live for, but everything to die for, then why not do it? What's holding you back? I'll tell you what's holding you back. The unknown of what will become of you is your fear.

"I have no fear. Something inside holds me back."

It is your mind that holds you back. Not your spirit. I know your struggles. I've been there. I didn't have nerve enough to do it myself. Someone else ended it for me.

Cidal's question cannot come fast enough. Before he can open up his mouth, Mother Goddess disappears. Her voice comes through to fill his room: *You will figure it out. It will come to you.*

He has never been influenced by anyone in his life…past or current. He feels that it is much too late to be influenced by anyone or anything now. Regardless of it being natural or spiritual. His mind is set. He will do whatever, whenever, depending on which tide rolls his vessel.

His first notion is to lie back down to cut some extra zees. His head touches the pillow, and then he suddenly questions what time it is. Glancing at the clock: 6:33. Cidal snaps back up and refocuses. He grabs his mobile to see if it shows the same time. When he realizes they match, he jumps out of bed.

'Where did the time go? It was just around 5:23 not long ago.'

Being late for work is no option. He knows he is already on job arrest. Any late arrivals without a solid reason, any slip ups, he will be temporary out of the workforce. A quick wash-up, on with his clothes, grabs a small glass of orange juice, a piece of toast with strawberry jam, brushes his teeth, and off he goes.

As soon as he steps outside, Ms. Pearly sees him as she sits inside of her first floor window apartment.

"Looks like you already late," she says.

Cidal turns and glances at his watch: 6:53. "I got it covered. It won't take me long to get there."

"If that's what you think, then go on with it. Personally, I don't think you do."

"Thanks. If it's the rent you're worry about…"

"I already got a solution for that. Just throw you out if you can't pay no more."

He hears her, but doesn't pay too much attention. He situates himself on his motor scooter and takes off.

Ms. Pearly waits until he is clear and gone before she reaches for her mobile phone. She scans through recent calls and presses contact. The only number that shows without any name being attached to it. Which means this particular call is unfamiliar. After three rings, a man's voice answers.

Hello.

"Yes, this is Ms. Pearly from…"

Yes, I remember your previous call. I kept a close eye on your mobile number.

"Is our appointment still set for today?"

Yes, I believe so. Around 11:00 this morning, correct?

"I'll be here. Just pull up in the front. I'll be out waiting. You still have the address?"

Yes I do. So I'll see you around 11:00 then.

"Okay, sir. I'll be here."

Will he be there?

"No…not if I can help it."

You sure it's all right? I feel like an intruder.

"I'm in charge around here. I run the place. What I say goes."

Okay. I was just making sure. See you at 11.

"Good enough."

The call disconnects. Ms. Pearly breaks into a half-smile and nods to herself. 'I'll see how much he's worth. Probably ain't worth nothing. We'll see after a while.'

Cidal parks his motor scooter in the designed spot at Rising Falls Memorial Hospital. He rushes in and immediately heads for the time clock. He gets his card and swipes in. 7:02. He figures that a couple of minutes won't make any difference. There is leniency of no more than five minutes. So he thinks. 4:02 will be the time he swipes back out. So he plans.

With no manager in sight to monitor who is on time or not, Cidal hurries to his janitorial crib where all of his cleaning supplies are kept in a storage room. He puts on his scrubs and prepares for his daily routine of filling cleaning solutions inside the appropriate plastic spray bottles. Having enough clean rags, a feather duster, furniture polish, and a stainless steel canister are put on his cleaning cart. A mop bucket with floor cleaner solution filled with water, a dust mop, and a carry on straight broom and dust pan. He already has enough of paper towels and tissue paper for the restrooms to refill. He goes out to begin his duties.

From working at a slow pace with all the time to spare, two hours creep by. His mobile indicates a certain signal, letting him know which app it came from. He reaches inside his pants pocket to retrieve the message. Just what he thought. One message from the WeChat app. It can only be from one person… Wei Mei. Immediately, he reads it.

Notice short. To leave today. I find out. Boss tell me. To New York. You won't see. Sorry!

Cidal shoots a message back, asking her when she is leaving. Three or four minutes later, she responds:

Taxi take me airport 10:00.

This is unexpected. He never suspected that she would leave on the fly…a spur of the moment decision. Most likely, this is her boss' doing, and not her choice to move so quickly. Doubts prick his mind that he may not see her again, if ever. The escort business is very unpredictable. Women come. Women go. They appear; they disappear, and then reappear. Time and time again. He needs to see her before she takes off. He looks at his watch. It is 9:08. He decides to put everything on hold. Stashing his cleaning cart until it's tucked away, so it would not be in the way of anyone's path. He makes a quick dash to his manager's office. Luella is not there. She is nowhere near or around her office. As he walks down the hall, he spots a coworker.

"Hey, have you seen Luella?" Cidal asks.

"No. Haven't seen her all morning," a male coworker replies. "Quite unusual. I always see her, but not a peek of her all morning. I'm sure she'll pop up sometime. Whatcha need?"

Cidal hesitates. He does not know if he should indulge any personal business to someone he barely knows. Besides, he is aware that most coworkers have been informed about his work habits and behavior. Not knowing what to do, Cidal just stands there.

"So? What is it? What's it gonna be?" the coworker asks, looking strangely at Cidal.

"I don't know. Just if you see her, tell her I was looking for her. That's all."

"All right. I'll give her the message when or if I see her."

"Thanks."

The coworker watches Cidal walks swiftly down the hall. He shakes his head in disgust. 'Crazy bird if I ever saw one. Ain't no tellin' what he wants. If I even see her, I shouldn't tell her nothing.'

He turns the corner and continues down the hall, but only half way. Cidal knows time is valuable. The minute hand on his watch inches closer and closer to 20 past 9. This is the point where his degree of not caring of the outcome; the carefulness of any results from his own actions becomes second hand. On a whim, he heads down the corridor back to his janitorial crib, changes out of his scrubs, leaves the area, and exits out of the hospital.

19

Racing through the busy streets of Rising Falls, but constantly aware of other vehicles and traffic laws, Cidal zooms on his motor scooter with an eager attempt to get to the hotel in time before Wei Mei can slip away. Stopping and going in the mid-morning congestion, he refuses to even glance at his watch. He is trying to get there as fast as he can, so there is no need to keep check on his progression. His mind is of one track. To see her. To be with her one last time.

Wei Mei is already packed and sitting on the side of the bed. Her coworker friend, Xia, comes into her room speaking Chinese at a rapid pace, urging her to get hopping. But she seems not to be in any hurry. She continues to wait…glances at her watch, and then she checks to see if there are any missed messages on We-Chat. There is none. Her friend stands with a continuous glare.

It took him all of 20 minutes from workplace to hotel. Finally, Cidal gets to the entrance, drives in, and parks where he normally does. The time is 9:45. With less traffic, he would have arrived 10 minutes earlier. There is no time to lose. He sends a WeChat message to Wei Mei. He waits for her response.

Two minutes go by. And then five. Slowly ten minutes winds the clock. Five minutes before 10, he forces his move to hit the path to go towards the hotel. As soon as he enters, he knows exactly where to go without any dilly-dallying. His pace is quicker than a stroll, but not as fast as a power walk. He stands in front of room number 128. Without hesitation, he knocks. Immediately, the door swings open to his surprise.

Wei Mei stands with her suitcase in hand. She is caught off her guard as much as he is.

"Ni hao," he greets her. "I thought I was too late."

"Ni hao," she replies.

Xia walks around from behind the door. She speaks Chinese to Wei Mei, and leaves the room.

"Bye," she says to Cidal, walking pass him. One of maybe two or three words she knows in English.

"Zai jian," which means good-bye, he responds in Chinese which is just as limited.

The door remains open. He steps inside the room. "I'm glad I caught you in time," he says to Wei Mei. He has no sign of her emotions, since she is practically stone-faced about his sudden entry. She then lightens up.

"I happy too," she says. "I go to airport now."

Cidal closes the door for a moment of privacy. Her suitcase is still in hand. He takes it out of her hand and sets it on the floor. He embraces her; she gives it back to him equally. A kiss is planted on her lips.

"I don't want you to go," he whispers in her ear, still holding her tightly.

She whispers back. "I like your hug. I like your kiss."

They pull away, standing, looking into the eyes of the other. "Taxi wait. I go." She picks up her suitcase.

"Wait! When can I see you again?" he asks.

"I don't know. I don't know I come back. Only boss tell."

He grabs the handle of her suitcase while her hand is still on it. "I'll carry this for you."

"No, thank you. I carry. I go now. Wait to come out."

Not really knowing what she means, Cidal stands and watches her leave the room. She leaves the door open and disappears. One minute goes by. He makes his move. Rapidly he heads down the hall and rushes to the main entrance. A cabdriver closes the trunk after putting in the last piece of luggage. At the very same moment, Cidal sees Wei Mei climb into the back seat of the taxi. Her friend, Xia, is already seated inside. She closes the door of the back passenger's side. The driver whips around and hops into the cab. Right before taking off, Cidal walks out. Wei Mei spots him. The taxi starts moving. She raises her still hand to the window. She carries no facial expression. The distance between the cab and Cidal increase by every second. He does not know how to react, so he does nothing but stands with his clothes moving from the gush of wind by the car.

This is all no big deal to him. It would be nice to continue physically with her. But the call has been made out for her temporary placement elsewhere. So he accepts it and moves on. Back to his motor bike. Back to work.

Manager Luella journeys through each floor of the hospital

checking on workers and catering to any concerns they may have. Once she gets to Cidal's area, she notices he has been there by the cleaning cart he left stashed away. She thinks nothing of it, walks through without a change of pace. Eventually, she runs into the last coworker who has seen Cidal. Right before she speaks with a morning greeting, he catches her in an open-mouth, silent breath.

"Hey, Luella! Mister Crazy was looking for you."

"Oh, yeah? When?" She stops.

"Funny, you know exactly who I was referring to."

"It can only be one Mister Crazy around here. But I shouldn't say that. I'm supposed to be objective rather than subjective. I have to toe a neutral line. What did he want?"

"Beats me. I tried to ask, but he wasn't upfront with anything. Just thought I'll let you know."

"Okay, thanks. Maybe our paths will cross. If not, I'll make certain to force a near-collusion."

"I hope I'm around when it happens. I would like to look in on that."

Luella does not respond. She walks away as though on a mission. Her business-like posture; her revved up anticipated demeanor all geared for a possible clash of the unexpected. While she attends to her responsibilities, going from one station to another, and then back to her office to immerse in her other duties, Cidal arrives back at work. He checks his watch. Little past 10:30, but not yet 10:35. He strolls back into the building as casually as he walked out more than one hour ago.

Everything is still in place, his cleaning cart and supplies are where he kept stashed. No concerns weigh on his mind. He puts on his scrubs and goes about his business as though he has been there all along. Five minutes into his cleaning, he hears the voice of his manager.

"Cidal."

He turns around to Luella. "Yes?" he answers.

"I understand you were looking for me earlier."

"Yes, at the time, but I no longer need to see you."

"Oh, is that so? Well, I need to see you immediately in the security's office." Luella leaves without explanation of what she may want from the private meeting. Cidal, once again, puts his duties on hold and goes into the direction of security.

Many thoughts flash through his mind. Security? What for? He knows he has not stolen any merchandise from the hospital or meddled in the affairs of other materials outside of what he is responsible for. Because of the recent lack of memory; sometimes not being aware of the passing of days and times, Cidal is hoping that he has not forgotten himself. To subconsciously participate in an act that he would never consider doing in his alert conscious mind. This bothers him.

Luella is waiting. A security guard who is on shift waits also as Cidal walks into the room. There are several TV monitors posing as eyes of the Almighty spying on every inch of the outside surroundings and throughout each corridor of the building. Luella asks the security guard to replay a pre-recorded activity from earlier that morning. He works the monitors to rewind and playback. Cidal is seen checking his mobile device; setting his cleaning cart in a designated area; talking to a coworker; walking into his crib storage room; walking out without his scrubs on, and then existing the building. Luella stares at him.

"Do you deny your actions?" she asks.

"There's nothing to deny," he says. "The security cameras show me doing my work."

"And walking out of the building," Luella adds. "Two hours into work, there's proof that you left without proper notification. Do you know what this means?"

"No, I can probably guess."

"Report to my office."

Cidal walks out and down the hall. Luella thanks the security guard for his time and his attention to details. She leaves the room.

He is already sitting in her office when Luella arrives. She closes the door for their privacy. She goes behind her desk and takes a seat.

"What you did is call for your immediate dismissal. Give me one reason why you left work without informing me. Not only that, you did so without even swiping out. All of this caravanning at the company's expense. I'll wait for an emergency reason or excuse. I'll be the judge on which one it is."

"I have no good reason to satisfy you. Only an excuse."

"Which is?"

"I needed to see someone off before leaving town. I just found out minutes before I decided to leave work."

"If this is so, how come you didn't ask permission from me? Instead, you disappear without telling anyone that you were leaving. This is also a security issue. All employees have to be accounted for while presently working and on the clock. If this was your first or maybe even second offense, there may be consideration. But it's not. This is one of many. I'm afraid you leave me with no other choice."

A luxury car drives into the parking lot of the apartment complex. Ms. Pearly sits in a lawn chair outside, waiting. The car parks in a space nearest the apartment building. Two distinguished African-American men wearing long sleeves colored dress shirts with opened collars and dress slacks. One is carrying an iPad in its case while the other is ending a call on his mobile. Ms. Pearly sees them and rises from her chair. She takes a step towards them as they approach.

One who has the mobile does the talking. "We're looking for Miss…"

"Pearly," she interrupts, "that's me. I'm the one you spoke to on the phone."

"Ahhh…yes. I'm Deeter Comptor, the curator from the Rising Falls Gallery of Art. This is my assistant, Promis. You explained to me there are some art pieces you wanted me to examine."

"Yeah. I have to do this when that no-good tenant of mine ain't around. I think he's wasting his time dabbling, pursuing foolish dreams. I want you experts to be proof that he is. Come this way."

The two men follow her into the building and up to the second floor. She selects one key out of many on her keychain and opens the door. They walk in.

"Here you go," she says. "A hodge-podge of pigsty splatter and scribble."

The men look at each other with no expression. They move in to a get closer view. Slowly, they examine each piece of art. Painting; drawings; completed and unfinished works. They remain speechless going from one to another. The one who has the iPad takes it out of its case and begins to snap still photos. He even video tapes every piece, scanning, taking his time. Ms. Pearly does not know what to think or how to ask it. She stands and observes, expressively in disbelief, doubting what she is witnessing.

"Y'all ain't saying nothing, but I see what you thinking." They turn and face her. "You gotta be kidding?" she says.

Cidal sits on a bar stool, pounding away drink after drink. Since his body is accustom to alcohol, his tolerate level is extremely high. He mumbles to himself. The bartender keeps a steady eye on him while performing his other duties. He is used to seeing people come in and plastering themselves into orbit. The difference is…this is late morning, on the verge of early afternoon. Way too early in the day to hammer down liquid frustrations.

"You okay, man?" the bartender asks.

Cidal vision is slightly blurred. But with two blinks, his focus is back on cue. "Yeah, I'm okay." He stares at the bartender. His ethnicity is hard to place. The bartender is muscular with a small ponytail in back. "What are you?" Cidal asks.

"Father black, mother Native American," the bartender says.

"Sorry, I usually don't ask such questions."

"That's okay. I get it all the time. Don't you think you had enough? It's early, man."

"It doesn't matter. Who am I? What am I? I'm nobody. Always was, always will be."

"That's the story of everyone's life. The ones who don't admit it are only fooling themselves."

"So what's your story?"

"Don't have one. I only serve drinks to people who do."

"Good enough."

"And what's yours?"

"Name something. Whatever it is, I'm sure I've got it."

Time crawls in millimeters. Cidal tolerate level becomes weaker and weaker. The bartender is one step ahead in the game. He stops serving him drinks.

"Look, buddy. You better get going. Where do you live?"

At this point, Cidal's speech is incoherent. He barely can remain sturdy on the bar stool. The bartender comes around, throws Cidal's arm around his neck and assists him to a table booth. He searches through his pockets to find his identification. Once he discovers where he lives, the bartender shoves his wallet back inside Cidal's pocket and returns behind the counter to call a taxi.

Groggy, not knowing his whereabouts, Cidal slowly begins to open his eyes. Through slits, he sees a blurry vision of a woman in front of him, calling his name, but her voice seems to be echoing from a distant tunnel. All of a sudden, from what he can see, a bucket of cold water splashes his face, forcing him half-way out of his stupor. He hits ground from the chair he is sitting in. He runs his hands over his face and opens his eyes to the surroundings outside of his apartment building with Ms. Pearly scolding him, holding the empty bucket. A cabdriver is getting back inside his taxi and leaves the premises.

"Drunk out of your mind," she continues to chastise him. "Whatcha doing getting drunk this time of day? You should be working."

Cidal steadily gets to his feet. He is still a little wobbly. His mind is foggy, spinning in a swirl of high liquid spirits.

"Can't work anymore," he tells her. "I gottta lay down. Ain't feeling too good." He walks towards the apartment, making sure every step is solid to keep his balance.

"In case you oughta know, two men were here earlier," she says. "I took them up to see that trash you been working on. So don't be surprised."

Comprehending what was said did not filter through. So Cidal decides to leave it right where he should. Under his feet. He tramples on. With great care, he climbs up to the second floor of the building, takes out his key, and as he is fishing for the keyhole, Ms. Pearly comes up behind him. She uses her own key to let him in. He staggers to the couch and plops down. She looks around the room. She glares at him.

"You're so drunk you don't even notice that some of your trash is gone."

Cidal barely can observe his surroundings. He shakes out the cobwebs from his head. "What happened? Where did they go?" Still not focused. Still not completely aware of anything.

"I told those men to get rid of them." She goes on to explain what she means, but Cidal does not hear her. He's still hungover. He heard all that he needed to. Being in a state of not caring, he closes his eyes and drifts into his own isolated world.

Potion B

20

He awakes from a long inebriation of spike juices and depression. There is a pounding on the door or is it in his head. He ignores it and closes his eyes. The pounding continues until it stops. Eventually, he knows he has to get up and stir around to get his mind and body functioning again. He is sprawled across the bed in his street clothes. By the natural lighting coming from outside, Cidal already knows it is past morning and into the afternoon. He glances at the clock on the nightstand. 12:37.

Slowly, he gets up and walks to the window to see what kind of a day it is. He notices two distinguished men that are not from the area walking away from the building and into the parking lot. Their attire…business casual. They get into a luxury car and leave. Cidal thinks nothing of it. He heads for the bathroom. He hits the shower.

He comes out with a towel around his waist, heading for the kitchen. His stomach grumbles for nutrients. Mother Goddess appears on the living room couch. At first he does not see her until she speaks.

You have no idea how I have worked. Your destiny now lies in your hands. What you do with it is up to you. Everything is set. The entire universe is aligned. But remember, in the end, your fate will remain the same.

Cidal is a bit taken back because of her unexpected arrival. And yet, he should be used to it. He tightens the towel around his waist to secure its covering. Mother Goddess giggles.

You don't have to. I've seen it all.

"You appear when I least expect it. What brings you around this time? My doomed fate? If you haven't notice, I lost my job yesterday."

Two and a half days ago. You were so drowned by alcohol that you misplaced a couple of days. You were fired on Monday. This is now Wednesday. According to your earthly timetable.

"It's no surprise. It's becoming a habit. I know. Don't remind me. I'm toeing the line between life and death."

Marvelous. You get a star for the day. She says with sarcasm dripping all over it.

"So this big thing you've been working on got me fired, huh."

No, darling. Your stupidity got you fired. But that's another issue. You can always get another cleaning job. People are always making a mess. It's job security. There are plenty of those types of work out there. But that's only a side issue. Your plateau has been raised. You will walk over the cliff and onto the sky without falling. You will continue walking across the sky only if you don't look down.

"What are you saying? What does all of this mean? Cliffs and all of this sky walking. I'm stupid. You have to break it down for me."

You will soon find out. The tide has turned. At least momentarily.

Cidal turns away to head to the kitchen. But then, realizes something. He turns back to speak to her.

"Oh, by the way…" He freezes. Mother Goddess is no longer there. Just what he figures. It's expected. He goes to wrestle up some grub for his starved body. Hot oatmeal, buttered toast, and a glass of orange juice.

He consumes his breakfast without hesitation. Once he is finished, he notices for the very first time that some of his art pieces are missing. He rushes over to search around the area to see if he has misplaced them. Behind portraits leading against the wall; canvases that are stacked in the corner, everywhere he looks they're nowhere to be found. This is the only room, the only place where all of his artistries are located. He panics. Then, through the dispersing, fading clouds of his mind he remembers Ms. Pearly's statement when he was deep in his stupor: "I told those men to get rid of them." Cidal cries out from the top of his lungs. Like a cannon, he blasts out of the living room, into the bedroom, throws on some fresh clothes, and bolts out of the apartment.

A business card that was stuck between the door floats to the floor in a gush of excitement and wind. Cidal barely notices it when he runs past. He stops dead in his tracks and looks back before descending the stairs. He walks back and picks up the card. The type of business: Rising Falls Gallery of Art. Curator: Deeter Comptor. Listed are two phone numbers: a business and a mobile number. A physical address and an email address. With the card in hand, not taking his eyes off of it, he casually walks back inside his apartment and closes the door. He scans the room to see where he left his phone. He grabs it from the living room table and begins pressing buttons.

Two hours later, Cidal leaves the apartment building. As soon as he gets outside, he sees Ms. Pearly getting out of her car and walking towards him.

"Where're you on your way to?" she asks. She is never shy on being nosy. "It can't be work. It's too late and you been cooped up in that room for two days straight."

"How come you never told me about the men from the art gallery?" he asks.

"I did. You were so stoned-cold drunk, nothing could get through that plastered brain of yours. They took some of your paintings, drawings whatever. I said they can't be worth much. I wanted to know if you were wasting your time or not. Apparently, those men took enough of an interest to take them with them. After I insisted though. They wanted to wait to talk to you and get permission. I told them a lie. I said I was a relative and it was okay. I'm glad I did. You coming in here higher than a kite on a windy day, all soused up with all that liquid filled up inside you, ain't no telling what they may have thought. I did you a favor. You better appreciate it."

"How did they ever find out about my work?"

"I got a few connections. I know a few folks. You weren't gonna do nothing. So I did it for you."

"Believe me I've been trying."

"I'm sure you have. It's all on who you know."

"I'm going to the art gallery now to see this Deeter somebody. I guess I got you to thank."

"It ain't no big deal. Me personally, I think it's a whole bunch of nothing. I guess I could be wrong. Somebody's seeing something out of it. I don't know what they're looking at, but they're seeing something…I guess."

"I'll let you know what happens if anything."

"You lost your job, huh?"

"Got fired."

"I figured that much. It was only a matter of time." She leaves him standing there while she heads towards the apartment. She turns back to him to say one last thing. "Oh, yeah! As you probably haven't noticed, your motor bicycle is back here. The bartender made sure to have it brought back." She disappears inside for good.

It is obvious that someone is looking out for him. Without much thought to pampering circumstances, Cidal hops on his motor scooter and heads out.

When he arrives at the art gallery, he double checks to see if the address is correct and to remind himself who to ask for once he walks in. The receptionist asks him if she can help him as he walks up to the front desk. Cidal gives her the business card. She glances at it and hands it back. She directs him to take a seat and she will have the person paged by phone. Moments later, a man comes to Cidal with his hand extended.

"Hi, my name is Deeter Comptor. You must be Cidal."

Cidal stands and takes a step forward for the greeting of a handshake. "Yes, I am. Glad to me you."

"I would like to have met you at your place of residence, but your aunty said you were not available when my assistant and I visited the first time. Then this morning, or shall I say early this afternoon, you were also not available. I knew it was short notice to just pop up, so I left my card inside your apartment door."

"Yes, I almost passed it when I opened the door, but luckily I was able to spot it."

"Very good. Come this way. Let me tell you all about our art gallery and why my sponsor and I are very interested in your work. Your aunty gave us permission to take several pieces of your art. Usually, we're not accustomed to doing that. But it seems like your aunty knows people who knows other people. It's a small world that surrounds this not so small city."

"Yeah. You can say that again."

Deeter goes on to explain what they actually do at an art gallery, and also the purpose for it.

"An art gallery is to exhibit the works of an artist. It houses various artworks including paintings, oil canvas, acrylic paintings, watercolors, ink drawings and other types of drawing. Also sculptures and wooden carvings. Our purpose is very commercial. We are in the business to promote the works of artists and to introduce them so they can sell their art. People come into art galleries with the intention of getting to know the artist's work and possibly to buy some pieces. We are funded by individuals or organizations to earn a profit. Specifically, our gallery is funded by a wealthy woman who has an appreciation for the finer things in life that doesn't always get recognized. Her late husband was an art collector. She wanted to do her part by displaying and showcasing local artistic talent here in Rising Falls. If you know the history of our city, you should know that we have a very rich renaissance culture that dates back into the late 19th and early 20th century."

"Oh, yes," Cidal says. "I'm very familiar with that. Who is the woman that funds the gallery?"

"Her name is Lady Ila Furren. She prefers to be called Lady Ila."

"Lady Ila? How do you spell it?"

"I-L-A. Pronounced I-la. She is quite unique and original."

"I see. Will I ever meet her?"

"Believe me. You will. She has a hand in everything around here. She lets us run the business end of things, and she doesn't get in the way. Although she is behind the scene, she's in control. At the same time, she is a very nice person. Easy to get along and work with. She doesn't allow her riches to go to her head."

Continuing to stroll through the gallery and into his office, Deeter explains to him what is expected and what will happen next. He asks for information in how to be reached and everything pertaining to the business end.

"Let me be very clear," Deeter says. "Lady Ila has the final say in everything. Nothing is done without her approval. So whatever is done is done with her fingerprints on it."

The many disappointments Cidal has experienced up to now are beginning to convert into opportunities. Events are on the verge of taking shape, setting him up for his ultimate challenge.

Outside of the art gallery, on his motor scooter, hitting the road, Cidal heads home with a feeling of optimism. He parks his bike and climbs off. Ms. Pearly sits inside her apartment window viewing the whole scenario. She does not wait. She meets him slightly outside of the entrance door of the building.

"So how did it go?" she asks.

"I guess it went okay. The curator seems to be interested. But we have to see if Lady Ila will go for it. The curator seems positive that she will. I have to see it first before I believe anything. You know how things like this goes. I ain't getting my hopes up sky high just for a crash. I gotta keep it on the ground."

"I'm sure it'll work out. Those two men were interested. I still don't see why. But they were. I guess anyone can throw anything together and call it art. And I ain't saying that all of it's bad. You may have one or two good pieces. That's all in my book. Maybe that's why I ain't no art lover. I would be a terrible critic. Or maybe I would be a pretty good one. I wouldn't mess around with no junk pieces though."

"Again, I'll see what happens, if anything."

21

Spells of depression come and go. Cidal is caught between two extremes. High expectations confront the lows of realization. If nothing comes from his artwork, he has to prepare himself for any type of work. He searches the newspaper ads for cleaning positions or any menial job that he can quickly land. His concern is keeping a roof over his head and enough food on the table. To avoid full concentration on his current situation, he explores the potential of feminine connection.

He converses with Wei Mei through WeChat. Asking her how she is doing, and letting her know that he misses her. Surprisingly, she engages in mutual dialogue by expressing to him how she wishes she was back in Rising Falls with him or him being in New York with her.

> *You come New York visit me?*
> *Can't get away now. Things are changing. But I would like to. Send me a picture.*
> *You like me?*
> *Yes I do.*

Ok. I send photo.

I can look at you when I can't see you.

On the verge of asking her how business is, his second thoughts keep him from asking. Does he really want to know or is it just small talk? He declines. He can care less in knowing. As long as she is happy, he is okay with it.

To get back the small pieces of his mind, Cidal continues the portrait that he started not long ago. The mysterious painting of his lady acquaintance…Wei Mei. Working a good portion of the day, he decides to escape for a bit to take in breaths of fresh air and a change in environment. By foot he leisurely breezes through the crowded streets of town and into the not so busy quieter areas of parks and walkways. He rests on empty benches. Still searching for that certain idea that would galvanize his art. Because of recent events, he is inspired even more to put his foot on the gas pedal. Out of the clear blue, his mobile phone rings. He looks at the number. Private. He usually does not answer private or blocked numbers that call him. Most often the calls come from another state or telemarketing businesses wanting to sell something. Anyway, a lot of these calls have absolutely nothing to do with him. Like most people, he would not be interested.

But this time it is different. There is an urge to see what this particular call is. So he takes his chances to answer with great hesitation.

"Hello."

Hello. May I speak to Cidal Sewell? A woman's voice is on the other end. Feminine, dignified but also with a very confident tone.

"Yes, this is him speaking."

Well, hello darling. This is Lady Ila Furren. We haven't met, but I've heard quite a bit about you. I'm the main sponsor of the art gallery. I believe you've met Deeter the curator.

"Oh, yes. I had a chance to go to the gallery and meet him. He showed and told me all about how the process works."

Very good. Well, listen hear darling. I'm not too much of a phone talker. I rather do my business in person. I would love to meet you. I feel you have a unique talent. I want to meet the artist behind the work. Are you free tonight?

"As a matter of fact, I am."

Splendid! I have your personal information Deeter gave me. I'll have a car to come pick you up. Does 7:00 work for you?

"It sure does."

Great! Sorry for the short notice. I just happened to call you on a whim.

"Oh, that's quite all right."

Looking forward to meeting you.

"I am too."

Wonderful! Good bye.

"Good bye."

After the call ends, Cidal sits; a gush of positive vibes running through his veins. A break like this does not come around often. Ceasing the moment and taking advantage of a once in a lifetime opportunity becomes his primary goal. With this, he will shoot for all that is in the bag and then some.

'Wow! It's a good thing I answered that call,' he says to himself.

"And what call is that?" a voice comes from behind. And it sounds all too familiar to him. He slowly turns his head to see Blue Beans standing with his hand on the top of the bench. He slightly leans in with one foot crossed over the other, with his toe pointed in the ground. "Care to expound?"

"Oh, it's you. As always, you're everywhere."

"Haven't seen you around lately. I was thinking you accomplished it."

"Accomplished what?"

"You know." In a knife like motion, Blue Beans slices his neck from ear-to-ear with his hand, indicating the obvious.

"I'm still here, ain't I?" Cidal says.

"Barely my good friend…but only barely. I ain't here to bother you. Just wanted to sees if you're still kicking. I sees that you are."

"You know everything, don't you?"

"I gets around."

"Where do you live?"

"You wouldn't believe me if I told you."

"Try me."

"In a tree house."

"That figures."

"See! I knew it."

"Okay. Where is this tree house?"

"In the forest, where else?"

"You're right. Stupid me."

"You said it. Not me. I gotta go. See ya around. Maybe."

Blue Beans goes on about his business, whistling. Well out

of earshot, Cidal says to himself, 'That guy. He's something else.'

Later in the evening, around 6:50, Cidal is casually dressed in slacks and a polo shirt. He mills around the apartment killing time, taking peeks outside his second floor window. He is looking forward to the meeting, but not overly anxious. He knows from prior experience that nothing is solid until the foundation is set. No pie-in-the-sky fantasy for him. His tree roots are firmly planted in the ground.

As the clock strikes 7, so does his pickup arrival as it slowly crawls into the parking lot of the apartment complex. A short limousine. A long luxury car. One of the well-known Japanese models. Cidal stands looking out, wondering if this is the ride sent by Lady Ila. A chauffer puts a foot down outside of the car, stands, and glances around. Cidal realizes this is it. He hurries out to meet him.

"Hello, sir."

"Yes, are you Cidal…?"

"Yes I am."

"I'm just the man you want to see. Lady Ila is waiting." The chauffer gets back inside. Cidal climbs into the back seat. The limo leaves.

Within city limits, on the other side of town, the limousine drives onto the property of a luxurious home. Something larger than a house, but a tad bit smaller than a mansion. The surroundings are pristinely manicured. Once the limo comes to a complete stop, Cidal gets out. The chauffer directs him to the main entrance of the house. He walks in to witness the elegance of the place. Nothing is out of the ordinary. Every single thing is stationed in its rightful position. By pressing a button on the wall, the chauffer summons a silent alert of notification.

Less than a minute, a nicely dressed female comes around the corner. She oozes femininity and elegance solely by the way she carries herself. She wears her maturity very well. Because of her beauty, it is hard to place a certain age on her. Fifty plus years…maybe, if not younger. Her ethnicity is even harder to pinpoint. Maybe sprinkles of African-American blood in her. It's very hard to tell completely. She is probably a mixed race of something other than Caucasian. Her hair is silky black with bits of small waves held up by an expensive hairpin. Her skin tone is between the shades of a dark olive to a medium brownish tint. She has her own unique speaking voice without any recognizable hint of an accent. Her smile radiates the room.

"Hello Cidal," she greets, walking towards him to share in a handshake. "It's nice to finally meet you."

"Thank you, ma'am. I'm glad to meet you too."

"Oh, please not that. Ma'am doesn't fit me at all. Lady Ila… Lady…or just Ila."

"Lady Ila seems to be what you're called according to Deeter."

"As strange as it may seem, people get the misunderstanding that Lady is a title. Well, in my case, it isn't. You see Lady is my first name. My given name. Ila is my middle name. So people assume when they call me Lady Ila, they are referring to some royal title. This isn't true."

"Well, I will call you Lady Ila. It has glamour. And so are you."

"Aren't you the flatterer? Thank you very much. I see we are going to get along very well."

The chauffer knows not to bud in. Without clue or signal, he dismisses himself, going back outside. No words are spoken.

"Come," Lady Ila says, "let's get more acquainted. There is a room where we can sit and talk."

She walks ahead of him, leading him into a room that is stylish and yet comfortable. Not big enough for a party or large dinner guests, but the intimacy suits the privacy of casual conversation.

"May I offer you a drink?"

"No, thanks. I might forget where I'm at."

She laughs. "You have such a good sense of humor. One small drink wouldn't hurt." She walks over to a small bar, whips out a couple of drinking glasses, and pours delicate, high spirits half-way full. She brings them over and hands him one. "Please sit," she says.

"You have a nice place. I'm sure it's expensive to keep up."

"It's okay, if one likes luxury. It's really not a big deal. Since I'm fortunate enough to afford it, why not? If it's available, take it."

"I wished I could be in the position to take things or leave them. Even if I could have my way, it still probably wouldn't change my struggle. But I'm willing to give it a try."

"What struggle are you referring to? Financial struggles are the only struggles known to our society. Fix those, then all would be well."

"Yeah, in certain circles, maybe, but not in my world."

"You are very fascinating. This is why I asked you to come. I want to know the real artist and his world. A struggling artist has a different perspective than an artist on easy street. I have sponsored artists who come from well-to-do families. Meaning, they can do anything else in their lives but they choose to use art as a pastime. They can take it or leave it. Their money supports them. But someone in your situation is totally different. Art is not a hobby. It's your whole being. The reason why you exist. You can't put it down and walk away from it. If you did, it would drive you insane. This is the artist I long to know. If my analysis of you is incorrect, please stop me."

"No, you're doing pretty good. You have me pegged."

"Not quite. That's just the surface. I haven't begun to see the real you. Deep inside, you have multiple phases of your existence. It's difficult to pinpoint one."

"Maybe this is true. I don't know. Maybe it's stereotypical of what artists pretend to be. I don't know that either. I believe I would be the same even if I was a surgeon. Tore up from the floor up."

She laughs again. "You are marvelous. Very humble…unassuming. You really don't know how much talent you possess. I have viewed your work. I fell in love with it. Not only what's on the canvas, but what's behind the canvas that makes me hunger to find out what's inside the artist."

They take sips of their drink. She looks at him curiously. A glint of inquisitiveness lingers in her eyes. He picks up on her vibe. He does nothing but remains cool. Never to initiate. Keeping himself open to whatever.

"I have to confess to you," she tells him. "I did something very naughty. I stole some of your paintings. I have them here at the house."

"I was wondering who had them," he says. "I thought Deeter from the gallery had them there. He never admitted if he did or not."

"Did you inquire about them?"

"I brought it up. All he told me was to not worry. That they were in safe hands. I let it go at that."

"I want to share something else with you." She takes another sip of drink. "I want to sponsor your work. Many pieces of your work. I want to introduce you as an unknown, coming of age artist who lives among everyday people in the same town, on the same streets that many of the forgotten ones reside on. It will take lots of work and dedication which you have already displayed. In other words, I want to take you under my wing and promote you to art lovers and dealers for profit. I have all the connections. Your work has tons of potential if the right eyes see it. I'm able and willing to make it happen for you."

"That's wonderful! I can't thank you enough. When does it happen? How do I go about doing it?"

"Leave all of that to me. Your only responsibility is to follow my lead. Do what you do best. Which is creating art. And do what you're told. If you do those two things, there will be no problems. I may even ask you for favors."

This time he takes more than a sip. He finishes his glass. She watches him from over the rim of her glass with that very knowing expression of what is behind her eyes. He acknowledges her stare with a glance of his own. He is reading her mind. More importantly, he hopes she is reading his. There is a concern. He wants to address his current situation.

"Yes, darling?" she says as a figure of speech and not as flirtation. "Something on your mind?"

"Yes. I was thinking what you said about asking me for favors. I might need one myself. It's more of a need than a want."

"Yes, dear. What is it?"

"When is the premier of my work?"

"Sounds like you're anxious to get started. I can arrange it in two or three months if not sooner. You're already ahead with the work you've produced so far. Why do you ask?"

"Well…" Cidal hems and haws trying to find a way to ask without appearing to be too demanding. "Well…let see…"

A flash of insight pricks her brain. She realizes what he is hinting at.

"Oh, forgive me, hon! How silly of me! You need compensation to live on. Am I right?"

"Yeah, something like that. I wouldn't ask for anything. But you see I'm searching for another job. Until I can get paid, I'll need a loan from you."

She laughs a little. He looks seriously at her. "Please, please don't misunderstand, darling," she says. "I'm not laughing at your need for money. What's so comical is that you feel the need to pay me back. Nonsense! Wait right here. I'll be back in a minute."

She gets up to leave the room. Just exactly what she said, she was back within 60 seconds. She sits back down beside him with a pen and checkbook. She scribbles out an amount and signs it.

"Here you go, hon. I hope this will be sufficient enough."

Cidal takes the check and looks at it. A quick inhale of breath almost knocks him out.

"Is there anything the matter?" she asks.

"No. I mean, maybe. There's no way I can pay back this amount."

"Again, no need to pay me back."

"No, I'm serious. This is way too much."

"Darling, have you ever heard of royalties?"

"Yes, of course."

"I believe in your potential so much, you can consider this as a royalty check. Your art will payback much dividends. I know art. And as I stated before, I have connections."

"Thank you so much, Lady Ila. You won't ever regret this."

"I know. I have confidence in you. Keep creating. Stick to me in what I can do for you, and you'll be surprised that you will gain much more than that. I always get a return on my investment."

"I'll do whatever. What favors do you want?"

Her eyes are glued to his face. "All that you are," she says. "I want to know all that you are. It's still early. I have enough time to find out. Are you hungry?"

He looks at her with a slight smirk, but remains speechless.

22

With his large royalty advance, Cidal is able to pay for his current and backed up rent. Ms. Pearly is more than willing to accept. He has never been in possession of this much money in his entire life. Regardless of the lack of funds in previous times, Cidal watches every cent, overly stretching the dollar. This is no time to get crazy and go on unnecessary splurges. Although Lady Ila has complete confidence in his artistic abilities, there remains in him doubts about what he can or will accomplish. Artists of all kinds go through highs and lows in their attempt to create something out of nothing. He knows this. The pressure of expectation is a rising tide.

He works on portraits day-in and day-out. After finishing one, he immediately jumps into another. Or he tries to complete those unfinished works left untouched. The time he takes off…sleeping, eating, and an occasional stroll throughout town.

A lonely lifestyle of self and art. Seldom does he interact with anyone. With Ms. Pearly…only in passing. He sends We-Chat messages to Wei Mei. They converse on occasions but nothing near consistency. The urges of his manhood needs a quick fix. By mobile device, he searches certain ads on a particular website to see perhaps ladies of an underground profession. The same ad from the same agency that he called previously when he first met Wei Mei is still advertising. They maneuver Chinese escorts in and out of town to freshen up their business. Cidal does not want to take a chance to hook up with some other girl just in case she knows Wei Mei. Even though they are not in any relationship, there may be one possible in the future.

On his laptop, he ventures onto China Romance Select. He scans through the website in search of a potential mate. There are women who did not respond to his prior messages. As a matter of fact, they did not think it was worth their while to even read what he had to say. No surprise. No problem. He moves on. Sending new messages to different women, dishing out heart interests to them, he can only hope to get a response.

Unexpectedly, one early evening, Lady Ila calls. This time it wasn't a private number. She has given him access to her number where he now has in his contact info. Her name appears on his mobile screen.

His hands aren't clean enough for him to touch the phone. He quickly washes and dries them off. Some paint remains on the back of his hand, but that doesn't matter. He rushes to his phone but by then it's too late. He calls her back without delay, trying to beat her leaving a voicemail message. Two and a half rings, she picks up.

"Hello." He speaks first.

Hello, darling. Busy?

"Just touching up a portrait I started months ago but never finished. Why?"

Dinner on the terrace. My place. Are you free?

"Yes I am. I need a break anyway."

Wonderful! In about an hour, my car will pick you up.

"Okay. I'll be ready." The call ends.

Exactly an hour later, Cidal walks out of the apartment building. Ms. Pearly is out and spots him. She sees the chauffeur driving up. Her eyes and imagination are keen, so she's able to put two-and-two together.

"Fancy company you're keeping nowadays," she says. "Your art must be selling or you're selling her."

"What does that mean?" he asks.

"You know exactly."

"She's my sponsor. She's gearing me up for an art show at the gallery. And how do you know it's a her?"

"Uh-huh. I wasn't born yesterday. I know what's going on. She dropped you off sometime last week. I saw the whole thing."

He chuckles. "It's not what you think."

"It's exactly what I think."

"Bye." Cidal gets into the car. Ms. Pearly watches as it leaves.

Arriving at the home of Lady Ila, Cidal is shown to the door by the chauffeur. The routine is already a habit. The door opens from the inside. Cidal walks in. Immediately, the door closes and he is greeted by the lady of the house.

"I'm happy you can make it on such short notice. I hate to disturb an inspiring artist while at work."

"Anytime I can take a break and be in good company, I'll always take it."

"Wonderful! Let's go out onto the terrace."

With her arm inside of his, she escorts him to a quaint table for two in the serene quietness of her surrounding premise. They have a seat. A cook comes out without cue and presents them with red wine from bottle to swirling glasses. He leaves and then returns pushing a rolling chart with two silver platters covered tops. He places both plates on the table, removing the tops. The piping hot aroma filters the private domain, ready to dig in to a delicious meal.

"Will there be anything else, ma'am?" the cook asks.

"No, thank you. Everything looks and smells tantalizing."

"You know where to contact me if you need something."

The cook quickly leaves. They begin without much conversation other than comments on how everything tastes. Gradually, the talk of business takes over. She explains to him how the process of art exhibition works. Through her connections, the word is already out about him and the excitement of the upcoming event. Cidal absorbs what she says. His response is very minimal. After going on and on nonstop of business talk, she cools her dialogue.

"Why, darling? What's the matter? Is there anything wrong?"

"Oh, no. Not at all. Why?"

"Am I losing you with all of this talk?"

"You're not losing me at all. I'm hoping I don't fall flat on my face. Or should I say, I hope that my art pieces don't crumble before everyone's eyes. It would be a big disappointment. Not to me. But to everyone's anticipation. Mainly yours. After your investment in me, the last thing I want to do is to let you down."

She is touched by his sentimentality. She reaches across the table and lays her hand on top of his.

"You shouldn't worry, hon," she reassures him. "I have tremendous faith that you will be a success."

"That's what's got me worry. You believe in me too much. Don't get me wrong. I'm glad you feel the way you do about my work. I just…I don't know. There's something inside building me up for a major letdown."

"Let me ask you a question. I want you to answer me as honestly as you can."

"Okay."

"Do you think you have talent?"

"I love what I do. That might not be the same thing. I never felt that I was ever good enough. But yet, I always desired to make a living doing what I love. A pipedream."

"You haven't answered my question."

She waits for an answer. He looks at her. He looks away for a brief moment. Then back to her.

"Yes, I feel I'm talented. But no one else may feel the same way."

"Thank you. That's all I needed to hear. You believe in your work. But at the very same time, you struggle to find if you will be accepted or not. That's normal. My bets are a sure thing. I've never gambled without knowing the odds. Let me reassure you all will be fine."

"Don't get me wrong, Lady Ila. I'm not afraid of failure. My whole life has been such. The difference is that I failed on my own. No one else shared in the disappointment."

"I understand. I appreciate your concern. I know talent when I see it. And I know the tricky business of art society. You have given me your confidence. I will never build you up for a disastrous crash."

From the middle of the meal to the end, their conversation is light and playfully. Skimming the surface of innocent flirtation, especially on her part. Cidal is very careful not to be the initiator of such actions. Because he knows what's at stake. One false move could send him packing up all of his dreams and opportunities she has provided him with, never to return again.

They ease their way into a private sitting room. The same one as before. Small and intimate. Finishing up their wine. Conversation is a bit harder to come. They both find their tongues lying still. Then, curiosity summons her to speak.

"How old are you, if you don't mind me asking?"

"45."

"45? You don't look it. Maybe no more than 35. But not 45."

"Thank you." He declines to ask her the same even though he is more than curious.

"Have you ever been married?"

"No. Never took the plunge."

"I'm sure you have children."

"To your surprise, no children either."

"Wow, that's amazing from today's man. You're not bad looking. I'm sure you had ample opportunities."

"What about you? I know you've been married."

"Yes. My husband died several years ago."

"Any children?"

"One adult daughter. We're not exactly on good speaking terms. She's young and stupid. She'll come to her senses eventually."

"Does she live around town?"

"No. She lives in Boston with her husband. Poor guy."

Cidal does not know if he should laugh or what. He does nothing. Poker face. He only nods in response.

"But my life is so uneventful. My husband was 20 years my senior. I was a housewife and a mother. I didn't work because I didn't have to. But you…I'm sure your life has been the life of a typical artist."

"If you wanna call struggle as typical, I got that down to a science. It's been my major."

"Well, all of that is behind you now. You got positive things to look forward to."

She puts down her glass. She takes the initiative in putting his glass down too. Her hand gently touches his. He senses in her eyes her desire. She slowly moves in for a soft kiss on his lips. He allows it. Because he knows she is in charge. He is not willing to disappoint. Nor does he have any desire to. His body posture…his behavior…she picks up on through intuition.

She whispers, "Stay with me tonight."

"Okay," he says with confidence, but she detects a little hesitation.

"I won't make you. Do you think I'm too straightforward? I don't want to be alone."

"No, I think you're fine. I like that you don't play games. You get right to the point."

"Maturity has taught me that. Speaking of…"

He seems to know what she is hinting at. He cuts her off. "No. I don't mind that you're a mature woman. You're not forcing me. I want to stay with you. You're very attractive."

"That's all I need to hear. Let's not talk."

They continue to kiss passionately and yet patiently, without any rush, savoring the delicacy of the moment. The heat of her inner passion comes through her lips. She slowly leads her hand down his chest and onto his already raised excitement. This is her cue.

"Let's go to where we can be more comfortable," she whispers.

They gradually stand and walk hand-in-hand out of the sitting room, ascending the stairs to go into her bedroom.

23

Art dealers, art collectors, art lovers, and the like steadily pour into the art gallery to view the displays of Cidal's pieces. Deeter and his assistant are there to educate and direct the art enthusiasts of the recent display of the unknown, local talent residing in Rising Falls. Some have come from big cities in state and out of state, reeled in from an excellent source of advertisement and marketing.

Lady Ila waits patiently, constantly glancing at her watch, checking the entrance, hoping that her star attraction will soon show up. It is very unusual for him to be late for the biggest day of his life. Time ticks by. She walks into a private room and dials his number. It rings and rings. No pick up. The call shoots into his voicemail. She disconnects the call and tries again.

Cidal is still in his apartment. He is dressed casually, a nice casual, sitting on the sofa with half a bottle gone and a small glass in his hand. His phone sets next to him. When the call comes through again, he sees Lady Ila's name popping up on the screen. For the second time, he ignores it. Pours another round into his empty glass and pounds it.

As calm and graceful as she always is, Lady Ila becomes a little flustered. Not knowing if something serious has happened to him, she's two steps away from panicking. She dials a third time. On this try, she leaves a message.

'Hello, darling. Is anything the matter? You should have already been here. People are filing in. Everyone wants to see you in the flesh. I'm getting a bit tensed. This isn't like me at all. I hate feeling this way. Return my call immediately.'

Five minutes goes by. And then ten. Curiosity-seekers are impressed with what they are viewing. They speak in low tones among themselves. They pepper Deeter, the curator, with questions about whom the artist is, and when will he appear. Nervously, Deeter gazes at Lady Ila who stands in the background, looking elegant but unassuming, trying her best to remain low-key. A tiny nod and a slight shrug of her shoulders tell him the whole story. Cleverly, he is on cue to skirt around the issue, explaining to the host of art appreciators that they should realize how artists are, waiting to make a grand entrance at just the right moment.

Lady Ila gets a vibrating call signal from her mobile. She recognizes her chauffer's number. Hastily, she walks to a quieter area and answers.

"Where is he?" she asks. She listens for three seconds, and then ends the call. Fast pace stepping takes her from where she is standing to the front entrance. She steps outside and scans the parking lot and spots her car and chauffer who is opening the back door. Cidal steps out from the back seat. He sees Lady Ila and starts heading towards her. She walks to meet him halfway.

"Where have you been?" she speaks loudly. "You were supposed to be here at…"

"I'm sorry," he interrupts. "I had to take care of some business."

Standing directly in front of him, she can smell alcohol on his breath. Not reeking, but enough to know he's been nipping.

"Are you drunk?"

"Not even close. It takes more than a few shots to get me staggering."

"Here, take my arm." Instead she puts her arm around his and escorts him in.

No grand entry is required. It doesn't fit either one of their styles. Once they immerse themselves in the company of others, people start to notice the bond between the two. Always close within a few feet of each other. She never lets him stray too far away. When one asks about the arrival of the artist, Deeter directs their attention to Cidal, who is trying to be invisible to a very visible crowd.

"The artist is standing among us," Deeter announces. "I would like to introduce to all of you, Cidal Sewell."

There is appreciation on the faces of those present. Lady Ila hasn't a clue on how Cidal will react to such attention. She remains close at hand to glue the pieces back together in case things fall apart.

He is besieged with questions and comments, handshakes of greetings. Lady Ila is approached by some of the top art dealers around, asking her where did she ever find such talent. She has known these dealers for years and is on a first name basis.

"Lady, you did not disappoint," one dealer comments. "You have a skilled eye for such pieces of work. Where have you been hiding this artist?"

She chuckles. "The art has to be good in order to catch my eye," she replies. "I have done nothing. All of the credit goes to Cidal. But let me warn you, he is very modest. He doesn't feel he has any talent at all."

Cidal becomes the center of attention. He is forced to indulge his inner works to those he has never seen before. Still within grasping distance, Lady Ila allows him to interact on his own, but constantly aware of her role of stepping in at the right moment if things go adrift.

The pendulum inside of him is unpredictable on how it will swing. Too low or too high on either side will create enthusiasm or lead to disaster. All because of his inner struggles he is always in conflict with, added with the liquid spirits that will abate or intensify his mood.

"There's nothing much to tell about me," he says to those listening. "Where do I get my inspiration? Who knows! I just create what I see from the images I receive from my brain. There is an ocean full of artists of all kinds that never get the recognition that they really deserve. Most are a lot more talented than me, if one even thinks I'm talented. Which I tend to disagree with. Because I feel I have no talent at all. I get enjoyment out of creating my artwork. I also get frustration out of the very same pieces. It lives and it dies all at the same time. Sorry, I'm not much of a talker.

Educated thoughts or words of wisdom never come from me. I'm simple and direct. No big deal. I'm glad you like what you see."

Lady Ila observes the reaction from everyone. She doesn't know what to expect from them. No one is turned off or offended by Cidal's lack of a documentary monologue. Frankly, they are slightly impressed by his wholesome candor.

The art showing of his pieces and social gathering continue on until late. His intro into the world of art is in its infancy, although his natural time clock is in the autumn. But as an artist, any artist, there is no time limit. One creates until one is dead. His painting utensils will never be put on the shelf. Retirement is not an option. Artists live in a different existence than those who lives depend on a certain structure of living.

The evening wears on.

Back at the home of Lady Ila, she and Cidal are laying on their sides facing the other in bed. Their conversation is barely a talk, but a whisper, setting the tone of their current mood.

"We were very successful tonight," she says. "When you arrived liquored up, you had no confidence in yourself or in me. Didn't I assure you everything would go well?"

"Yes, you did. I'm pretty new to the game. I don't put too much trust in other's opinions. I trust you, but not them. Art critics who pose as art lovers never gained my confidence. They're too fickle."

"Hmmm…and so are artists. I had no idea what to expect from you earlier. I felt I had no control if things down spiraled. All went well. They were impressed with you and your work. We make a good team."

"Yes, we do. How long will this keep up? Can I make a career out of one art showing?"

"As long as you can create like you do, I will always promote you. I do for you as you will do for me."

She leans in for a kiss. Slowly, the warm desire of intimate closeness begins to build. Her hunger for his sexual appetite is insatiable. Her passion is deeply rooted. She sends out a hard, silent gasp, anchoring him into the depths of her bearing.

Pillow talk resumes after the rush of climatic explosion descends. The hush of quiet voices, a word here, another one or two words there, eventually lullabies cradle them into a gentle overnight nap.

By morning, he is in bed alone. He wrestles in different positons catching the last drop of sleep. Her presence remains absent. He wants to keep good company status, so he gets up, washes in the adjoining bathroom, slips back into his clothes, and goes downstairs. Lady Ila sits at the dining room table on her iPad with a cup of coffee. She is in a short silk robe with the belt tied around her when he walks in.

"How long have you been up?" he asks.

She takes her eyes off the iPad. "Oh, good morning, darling. About an hour or so. Breakfast is almost done. I just got through communicating with Deeter and our business accountant. We made a lot more than I originally thought."

Cidal sits down at the table. "That's good to hear. It's amazing to me that people have that kind of money to purchase some paint thrown on a canvas."

She chuckles. "Your work is much more than splashed paint. You're always the modest one. I'll make sure you receive your portion of the royalties."

"Okay. More money coming into my hands? I'm forever grateful."

"What's on your agenda for today?"

"I'll probably go back home and continue on with my art."

"I see. Artists are constantly working on their next creation. Will you continue residing at your current residence?"

"Probably so. It fits me. It's affordable and quiet. I live alone, so there's no need to impress anyone."

"You mean no need to impress a woman."

"Well, maybe something like that."

She smiles. "I admit…we women are a lot choosier than men. Men can be comfortable wherever they choose to live."

"You may have a point."

She gazes at him as though she has something else on her mind. "I'm 55." She leaves it at that, waiting for his response.

"I don't say this to be cute, but you can pass for a woman much younger. You must have good genes. Fortyish, maybe. Not mid-fifties."

"Thank you for your kind words. I don't feel my age."

"You're also attractive and poised. That's a plus with any woman."

"Hmmm…you're sweet." There is a silent between them. She keeps her gaze on him. "I have a proposition. Why don't you live here? You'll have all the room you need. A large room for your artwork. Freedom to move about, you can come and go as you please."

"That's very nice of you." He pauses. "I don't know, though."

"I understand. You don't want to give up your independence as an artist. Well, think about it. Take your time. Once you decide, let me know."

"Okay. I'll think it over."

"You'll always have a place to stay. Stable resources. You wouldn't have to worry about financial issues. This can all be provided for you."

"Thanks for the offer. I'll keep it in mind."

"You're the only one I have ever offered this to. When I invest in something, I usually go all the way. If you turn it down, some other buck is not waiting in the wings. I've never competed, collecting male trophies. I just want you to know this is an exclusive offer."

"I appreciate the compliment. I will definitely consider it."

The door opens from the kitchen. Hot breakfast is served on trays. The morning cook is different from the evening cook. Cidal notices, but does not mention it.

24

Cidal receives an email notification through his mobile phone. In the middle of producing a new portrait, he hears the signal but does nothing to retrieve what might be only junk mail. His email signal is different from others on his phone. He knows it isn't a text message, a WeChat notification, or any of the other distractions. Whatever it is can wait.

With his concentration on his work, time slips away. Hunger rumbles his belly. He applies the minor touches before leaving his apartment to grab some dinner.

In no particular hurry, he takes an easy stroll down the street, hands in his front pants pockets. The climate, weather, and freshness in the air are agreeable to a mind that needs rejuvenating. His first thought is to stop at one of many eateries in town; in the mood for a delicatessen dish of some kind. His immediate second thought directs him to pay a visit to the small restaurant owned by uncle. Uncle Ease. It's been awhile since he last stopped in.

He isn't in his usual spot outside of his establishment. Cidal thinks out loud to himself, 'He actually must be working.' He walks inside and sees uncle behind the counter delivering instructions. He is quick to spot any patrons coming in.

"Hey, sonny!" he shouts out.

"Hello, uncle. Thought I drop in to have a meal."

"I believe I know what you want."

"You got it."

"It'll be ready in no time."

"Okay."

Cidal takes a seat at a corner table. Suddenly, he remembers the email notification that he forgot to check before. He whips out his phone, goes to his email carrier app, and searches his new message. The very first unopened email appears in bold print. It's from the Chinese Romance Select website, letting him know that one female member has sent him an interest and a personal message. A photo of her appears. One of the many women he initiated contact with has responded to him. She is actually the first and only response he has received in the many months of being a member. He will have to hold off until he gets back home.

Uncle comes over and speaks to Cidal. "What's the good word, sonny?"

"I wish I knew."

He sits down across the table from him. "Been keeping busy? Haven't seen you."

"Yes, you can say that. Painting and whatever comes my way."

"Oh, I see. You still single?"

"Yes I am."

"Huh! Couldn't find the nerve to do it? I get it. You're much better off. Didn't I tell you?"

"Yes I remember. Who knows what will happen."

"You still seeing her? That gal from China?'

"She left for New York. She may be back through here again."

"Yeah. You never can tell. Girls in that kinda business move around a lot. They're here for one minute and gone the next. Ain't too smart for a fella to get too caught up with them. I know they're women with emotions and thoughts and all of that. But they come in contact with a number of men. Most of the women can have their pick if they're looking for someone. I'm glad to see you haven't fallen for one. Or for anyone for that matter. Let them fall for you. You ain't heartbroken over it, are you?"

"Oh, no! Not at all."

"Good. I'll have to disown you as a customer if you had."

Cidal searches his eyes to see if there is truth in them. Uncle stares back. After seconds of seriousness, they both have a good laugh.

"I better get back. Here comes your food." Uncle gets up and leaves.

The server lays down the plate and asks if there is anything else he needs. Cidal declines. And then says, "Oh, yeah! Lemonade please."

He had his light conversation. He had his medium-sized meal. Now it is time for him to go back home and check the message sent from a prospect on China Romance Select. He turns the computer on. While waiting for it to fire up, Cidal brushes his teeth. He comes back and sits on the sofa with his laptop on the center piece table. He never sets his laptop directly on his lap. He is very skeptical. He does not want to take any chances that the heat from the computer could burn off sperm cells. Being in his middle forties, he wants to preserve as much of himself as possible. No low sperm count. In other words, he wants to be able to use it until he loses it into his older years.

He logs in and goes right into the inbox to read his message. It is all in Chinese characters. This website has a translation feature included. He clicks on translate. Below the Mandarin message, the English translation is available.

Hello Dear One,

I'm so happy to receive your interest message. I like your profile. I think we match up very well. I hope we can establish friendship first. Then, see what happens.

Yuli

This brings excitement to him. But a very subtle excitement. A practical mindset needs to be incorporated. He falls back on the philosophy of nothing will happen until it happens. He sends back a message to acknowledge the mutual interest they have in each other. This is the only response he has received from all the women he has initiated contact with. His intentions…to find out more of who she is and what she is about.

He revisits her profile on China Romance Select. Her main photo and other four pictures are favorable. Nothing out of this world. Just favorable. Enough for him. She is 32 years old. Her height is 5'4; weight 108; slim build. She has never been married and does not have any children. If she wants children one day, she indicates—undecided. Her occupation…other. There is other information that describes her in different categories. The one category that stands out to him is her religion. Christian. He knows that most Chinese do not fall into this particular religion. If any, they practice an eastern philosophy or do not participate in any structural religious faith. But because of the western influence of missionaries traveling the globe, there are those who have accepted the concept of Christian principles.

Under the section of what she is looking for in a mate, Cidal matches up well in what she hopes to find.

In the series of days, Cidal corresponds with Yuli from inbox to inbox on the website. Every time a message is delivered to him, he gets the notification from his personal email account, which indicates a signal on his phone app. Their corresponding consists of getting to know the other better. Their likes and dislikes. Things they like to do; places they like to go. What are they looking for in a relationship? So on and so forth.

Because of their different schedules, they do not communicate every single day. Every other day or every two days. The time also plays a part in when they do correspond. Her time in China is 12 hours ahead of his American Eastern Standard Time. This difficulty in keeping connected prompts Cidal to suggest another proposition to her. WeChat. When he asks her, she answers that she has an account. She is a bit surprised that he has one, considering this is a Chinese app for social networking. They accept each other as friends on their accounts.

Yuli becomes his second friend contact on WeChat. After the name Yuli, the word lawyer is inscribed in Chinese characters. With this mobile app at their disposal, they are able to communicate every day, as many times as they want per day. Just like he does with Wei Mei. Unless he shares events of his life in photos, articles, or whatever he wants to display in his discover moments, no one else can view personal messages from one user to another. Sharing in his discover moments means that everyone he is friends with can view what he puts out. Since he only has two friends on the account, he declines to show anything in his moments. He is in it only for person-to-person contact. However, he can see what his two friends share on their discover moments. Cidal is much more private and can care less about showing uneventful activities of his life.

Like a syringe shot to his arm, he is provided with temporary relief from the drudgery of the past work of cleaning at the hospital; the painstaking efforts of getting recognition for his art; the absence of a meaningful relationship with a female companion, and the inability to comfortably support himself financially. Recent circumstances have rendered these activities many miles behind him, and still there is something in him that keeps everything fresh in his memory. Being able to escape a few pitfalls in life does not mean that he is cleared from the struggles that plague him. The amenities to help support his life has gotten better, but his inner turmoil has remained. Not always present in the forefront of his mind, but it keeps lurking in the shadowy backdrop, waiting for the right opportunity to pounce on its prey once again.

To counterattack, Cidal keeps pushing his art. Constantly busy creating and finishing pieces. His schedule is off-tilted. Sometimes working throughout the day…morning, afternoon, and evening. Other times working the graveyard shift of midnight to dawn, catching sleep during daylight hours much like a mad scientist would do. A sweet or sour spot inside drives him to create different bodies of art paintings. When inspiration strikes, he presses the gas pedal to the floor completing pieces much faster than before and still is able to create art that is creditable.

On one of many absent days apart from each other, finally, there is a knock on his door. He finishes two-to-three strokes with the brush before getting up to answer. When he opens the door, Lady Ila stands waiting.

"Hello, my absent friend," she says.

"Oh, hello, Lady. Come in. I'm glad to see you."

She walks in and he closes the door. He gives her a hug. Ms. Pearly slowly pushes open her slightly cracked door from the first floor to look up the stairs in the direction of Cidal's apartment. 'Uh-huh,' she says to herself. 'There she is.'

"Are you really happy to see me?" Lady Ila asks with skepticism. "It's been several days."

"It has been. I've been busy painting. You've been busy too. Our calls or texts never connect when we're both free it seems."

"So this is your little hideaway." She looks around, slowly walking, moving about the room. "I've never been up here. Very quaint for an artist."

"Well, it's cheap for my lifestyle."

"Yes, darling. A lifestyle which has improved greatly for you. You now can afford to live anywhere else in town. But you remain here. I think it's very nostalgic to never forget the place where you've always belong. You know, my offer still stands."

"I'm still thinking about it. I'm so used to working and living here. By looking around you can see I'm very simple."

"It's very comfortable. Very unique." She sits on the couch and crosses her legs. "You're hard at work. Am I disturbing you? You want me to leave?"

"No, I'm glad you came. Just touching up a portrait."

A signal on his mobile lets him know he has a message. This particular signal is from his WeChat app. His first thought is Yuli from China Romance Select. His second is Wei Mei, Chinese escort. Since it has to be one or the other, he ignores the notification. His concentration is on Lady Ila.

"Text message?" she asks.

"No. Some notification from another app. You know how those things go. I'll check to see about it later."

Actually, he is dying to see who it is now. Even if he checks, he wouldn't be able to respond without tallying back and forth with whoever left the message. So he lets it be.

She sits there gazing at him, expressionless, not saying anything. He remembers his manners. He grabs a cleaning cloth on a table close to his easel and wrestles his hands in it, tosses it back, and gets up. Making his way over to the couch, he sits close to her.

"You've neglected me. A woman has her needs."

"I have the same needs. But manly."

He puts his arm around her. They kiss. She touches his face with the tips of her fingers, stroking him lightly.

"Don't get me wrong," she says.

"I have never misjudged you. You are too direct and straightforward in your approach to everything."

"Life is too short, darling. I've learned to enjoy what's important…what's really important. There is no price tag for it."

"That's refreshing coming from a woman as wealthy as you are."

"Money cannot buy health or happiness. I'm relatively healthy."

"Are you happy?"

"I'm most happy in the company of people I cherish. Giving back to the community. Doing things for charities."

"And what about my company?"

"I treasure your presence in my life. From a business and personal standpoint."

"I feel the same way. Without you…I don't know. My work would've never been discovered."

"The talent has to be there first in order to get the recognition. You laid the foundation and built the house. A beautiful house in the wilderness. I only brought the people out to see what has been in isolation. That's all."

"You're very modest."

"On the surface. But my desires are very bold."

Their passion heightens through the kiss. He gets up, takes her by the hand to raise her to her feet, and escorts her into his bedroom.

25

Very few times Cidal is ever spotted by Ms. Pearly. He remains quiet in his seclusion of the social climate that surrounds the city. He is either buried inside creating art or out privately somewhere. Never to know when he comes and goes, she keeps a close eye on his apartment waiting for the right moment to nab him.

One early morning before the dawn breaks into the day, by happenstance she peeks outside of her apartment window to witness Cidal standing by his motor scooter. She rushes out so she can catch him before he takes off. When she hits the front entrance of the building, she slows down as though she is casually stepping outside to get some fresh morning air. But Cidal is not leaving. He is walking towards the building as though arriving.

"Nowadays, you're always coming or going," she says. "Where've you been hiding yourself?"

"Just here and there," he says.

"She bought you, didn't she?"

"Who bought who?"

"Don't play dumb with me. I've been around long enough to know what's going on. That rich woman friend of yours. The one who's supporting you while you make love to her."

"She sponsors my art."

"That ain't all she's sponsoring, either."

"You need me for something? My rent is paid, correct?"

"Checking on you, that's all. I don't even think your artwork is all that special. She gave you a piece of money to hold you over. All of a sudden, these dealers come from out of nowhere to buy your trash. She's pulling a lot of string to keep you under her skirt. And you think you made it. Ha! I know what's really going on. She's clever. I give her that much credit. How much longer you gonna be here?"

"For the rest of the day. Working on art."

"I don't mean that. Living here? How much longer? I'm surprised she ain't got you shackin' up with her yet. Or better still, have you set up in some plush condo with all the amenities paid out of her banking account. One or the other will end up happening."

"I'll be here as long as I want. I can do my best work here."

"Best work my foot! In my estimation, you ain't done nothing. You throw some paint together and move around the brush. Masterpiece? Masterpiece my…" She stops herself from saying what's really on her mind and what's on the tip of her tongue. "Hold on! Is this a Sunday? I can't talk like that on the Lord's Day. But you know what I mean."

"I'm just getting started. More is to come."

"Uh-huh. You listen to me. You listen to me good. If you stop all of that funny business with that rich woman, you won't be making no more money with that so-called art of yours. She's only building you up so you can be her private gigolo. Women like her needs to be in control. Mark my word. If you tell her that you don't want to be her plaything anymore, she won't sponsor your work, and you'll be back to square one. She can pull all the strings to get her way. But yet I'm sure she acts real sweet and humble to you. Cross her up, and you'll see another side of her. All the doors to the art world will be closed to you."

"I'll see what happens."

"Yeah. You do that."

Cidal goes inside and walks into his apartment. He freshens up and gets a bite to eat. All the while, he keeps reflecting on what Ms. Pearly said. His memory jaunts back to what Lady Ila said to him on more than one or two occasions. Peppering him with thoughts of them making a good team; sautéing his imagination of asking for favors. He goes over the scenario over again in his mind.

'It can't be true what Ms. Pearly says,' he tells himself. 'Maybe there is something to it though.'

A voice rings out.

In life and in death, everything is possible.

Cidal gets up from the kitchen table and like a cool draft he enters into the living room. Mother Goddess is sitting in front of his easel viewing his current art project.

"Oh, you caught me off guard," he says. "At first I thought I was hearing things."

She never looks up at him. She keeps her focus on the painting, gently moving her hand over the portrait.

You are always hearing things. You can hear things that others can't.

"Where've you been lately?"

It's a big universe. I get around when I want to.

"Speaking of the universe, there is life on other planets, isn't there? I mean other existence in the galaxy in all of that."

She now glances at him. Then she looks back at the portrait. *How arrogant humans are on earth.* She looks at him again. *There are civilizations much more advanced than what can ever be possible on this planet. And there are those still developing.*

"Where do earth rank among those higher civilizations?"

Not everything can be measured with a scale. But for your earthly comprehension, 1 being the lowest and 10 being the highest, those advanced worlds are sitting at 10.

"And where does our civilization stand?"

3…maybe 3 and a half at best.

"It figures. I shouldn't be surprised."

The sad thing about it is this earth world should be much more advanced than where it is now. Narrow-mindedness and greed have hindered progress. It will eventually lead to its downfall.

"You know this to be true? That earth will collapse and fall?"

I have already said enough.

"What brings you around this time?"

Nothing.

"What? No warnings? No enlightening news or thoughts?"

Nothing. Nothing at all. You hold the key to all that you need. That one single key will open every door.

"And which key is that?"

The key your spirit possesses.

"Wonderful! What does that mean?"

You are a natural man. But you are more spiritual than you think.

"I don't get it."

You don't have to. Just keep living. Or in your case, half living. See you some other time.

"Wait!"

Yes.

"I didn't get a chance to thank you for setting things up for me. With my art opportunity and all. You said before you worked overtime. Thanks again."

She smirks. *Enjoy it while you can. Nothing stays the same.*

In one blink of an eye, she is gone.

Ms. Pearly is standing with her ear pinned to Cidal's outside door.

'I wonder who's he talking to in there,' she whispers to herself. 'I only hear his voice and nothing else.'

She hears him stirring around. She knocks on the door. Within seconds, he opens it. Ms. Pearly tries to look around him to see whatever she can.

"Everything all right in there?" she asks.

"Yeah, everything's fine. Why?"

"I hear you in here talking."

"Yeah, I do that a lot. I talk to myself."

"I always knew you were crazy. I'm gone." She turns to leave, and then for a split moment turns back. "Remember what I said about that rich woman."

"I will, I will."

"I'm telling you straight. You just remember."

"Okay, Ms. Pearly. Don't worry about me. I'll be fine."

"And you know what? It's a good thing you didn't go nowhere. If I was betting money, you'll be right back here where you started."

Finally, she leaves. Cidal closes the door and takes a deep breath. He tries not to put too much emphasis on what she said.

He sends out two messages on WeChat before sitting to continue painting where he left off. Fifteen minutes into his painting, he gets a signal back. He checks to see which of the two women responded. Wei Mei. And rightfully so. Once he reminds himself of the time, it makes sense. Wei Mei is in New York in Eastern Standard Time. The same time zone Rising Falls is in. This is late morning during the weekday. China's time where Yuli from China Romance Select is currently in puts her at 12 hours ahead late night.

He reads what she says. Then he responds to her. Back and forth.

I am good. And you?

I'm fine as well. Things are a bit better. How is New York?

You still like me?

Yes I do.

You come to New York?

How long will you be there?

I don't know. Maybe one month. Maybe two.

Will you come back to Rising Falls?

Up to boss.

Maybe I can come to New York.

Really? You come when?

I will check on the ticket. I will let you know.

I happy.

I'm glad.

You miss me?

Yes I do.

Ok. I wait you come to New York.

I will get back to you.

Ok.

He fires up his laptop computer as he paints. Online he searches for an available flight that is reasonable for short notice. A four-day getaway starting this weekend. He books the flight and immediately sends a message to Wei Mei.

26

Plans are made for a weekend excursion. Two different outings are planned for the same person.

Cidal has already booked his flight to take off to New York for mid-afternoon Friday. Wei Mei anticipates his arrival. Knowing he will not be engaged in any artwork during the long weekend, he tries to get as much painting done as he possibly can.

Thursday morning, more than 24 hours before his scheduled flight, Cidal gets a phone call. Half-asleep, half-awake, he reaches over towards his nightstand to see who it is. Lady Ila. He answers.

"Hello," he answers groggily.

"Good morning, darling. I hope I didn't wake you. You sound sleepy."

"No, I'm okay. What time is it?"

"It's 10:00."

"10:00? Oh!"

"Late night for you?"

"Yeah. I was up most of the night painting."

"That's the reason why I called. You've been working so hard lately that you need some time off. I arranged for the two of us to escape. There's a little cottage way out in the village that would be perfect for us to spend the weekend at."

"Sounds wonderful," he says, still trying to gain his faculties. "When do we leave?"

"Tomorrow morning."

"Okay." After several seconds, he realizes he already has plans for this upcoming weekend. This snaps him out of his haziness. He shoots into a position leaning on his left elbow. "Oh! Tomorrow's Friday."

"Yes, I know, honey. It's a nice long ride out there. I love long drives. We can take my car. You can drive. It'll take a couple of hours to get out that way. We both need a nice, long weekend getaway where we have everything to ourselves. You've already said it was a wonderful plan."

"I know. That's all good. But…"

"But isn't an option here, darling. We both need this. I won't take no for an answer. I hate being denied."

"What if I made plans already?"

"Very simple, sweetie---cancel them. You can always go back to whatever it is. This is important to us. You will not disappoint me, will you?"

"No, I guess I won't. I couldn't after all that you've done for me."

"Done for us. I benefitted also."

"Yeah."

"My car will pick you up later this evening and bring you here, so we can spend the night together. Then off to a fresh start tomorrow morning. Any objections?"

"No."

"Wonderful! I have things to do today to prepare. My car will drop by around 6:00. Don't eat too heavy today. We'll have dinner together when you get here."

"Okay."

"Talk to you soon. Bye."

"Bye."

He shakes his head and rubs his eyes, trying to get rid of any remnants of slumber. He clears his mind. Wondering what to do about his preplanned flight to New York to meet up with Wei Mei, he does nothing at the time. He gets up and rinses his face in cold water. In the living room, the finished work of Wei Mei's portrait sets on the easel. His signature of his first name is written at the bottom right corner. The portrait is silent and mysterious. Much like she is. The illumination of her eyes gives away her ethnicity. Her face is shrouded in a mixture of metaphysical and natural elements. He stares at it from different angles.

'I hope she likes it, but it'll have to wait,' he tells himself. 'She'll be disappointed that I'm not able to come. The sooner I let her know the better.'

Before doing anything else, Cidal calls to cancel his flight. When talking to his travel agent, he is informed that Southwest Airlines has a policy which allows a change of flight plans to be rescheduled at a later date within one year. This is welcoming news to him. He does not have to lose his money. He will notify the travel agent when he is ready to schedule again.

He sends Wei Mei a WeChat message: *Can't come this weekend. I'll make it up as soon as I can. Sorry!*

Replacing her portrait with an unfinished one, Cidal goes right to work without delay. An hour slips by. Still there isn't any word back from Wei Mei. He gets a message that sounds like the WeChat notification signal. He gets up and takes a couple of steps to retrieve his phone from the center piece table. Yuli from China Romance Select. Just like he has to do with Wei Mei's messages, he presses the Chinese characters and select translate for it to bring forth English.

Mistakenly, she asks him how his day was. He reminds her that she is in her night while he is into the late morning of his day. They both have a feel good exchange over the miscalculation of time. She shares photos of her daily activity of the day. Having dinner with friends at a circular turning smorgasbord of Chinese delicatessens; outdoor excursions and the like. And because his life is so uneventful, the only thing he can share with her are self-photos. Their conversation goes back-and-forth in no more than two minute intervals for a response. Eventually, she wants to sign-off to sleep. They say their goodnights.

By the time he hears from Wei Mei, it is already past noon. The exact timing is around 1:24. She sends her disappointment of his change of plans. He explains that circumstances a bit out of his control forces him to reschedule. He texts her through WeChat that he will try to make amends by the following weekend. She seems to be fine with that. By her tone, it's hard for him to make an accurate judgement on how she truly feels.

Taking a break from his work, Cidal escapes into the city, walking, collecting his thoughts in the attempt to refresh his brain. Far off down the street, but close enough for him to recognize Cidal in his leisure stroll, is Blue Beans sitting quietly on a bench, watching the flow of traffic and people. With a half-crazed look on his face, Blue Beans does nothing to get his attention. But he watches Cidal's every move like a hawk's tunnel vision. The closer he gets to him, the more Blue Beans' glare intensifies. Without even knowing he's being observed, Cidal quickly changes directions to carefully jot across the street to continue on his journey. Blue Beans never flinches. His eyes are still focused. Right before Cidal turns the corner to head down another path, he turns and shoots a look at Blue Beans, as though he knows all along he is being watched. A nerve strikes Blue Beans in the right spot and he bursts out into a loud, hilarious laugh. No expression is needed for Cidal. He slowly moves on and out of sight.

Around 5:30 in the late afternoon, he packs a couple of things in an overnight duffel bag to spend the weekend with Lady Ila. As always, the car pulls into the apartment complex at 6:00 sharp. Cidal steps away from the window, grabs his bag, and heads towards the door. Before walking out, he glances back one last time, making sure things are where they're supposed to be and that there isn't anything he's leaving behind.

He walks out of his apartment, down the stairs, and out of the building.

"Uh-huh," a voice sounds out.

Cidal turns and sees Ms. Pearly sitting on a swing patio sofa.

"Hi," he says to her.

"Hi? You mean bye. I know exactly where you're going. You hitching up with that rich woman. Look at you! Duffel bag and all for an all-nighter."

"I'm going away just for the weekend."

"I know. She's gotcha. And don't say it ain't true. You gonna be laying up with her. Uh-huh. I know."

"I'll see you when I get back." He walks towards the waiting car.

"She knows exactly what she's doing. And don't let her find out about that Chinese gal. If she ever does, your art career is over. She's only stringing your so-called art around for one thing. And you know what that is."

Cidal climbs into the back seat of the car and closes the door. The chauffer glances back at him.

"What is that all about?" the chauffer asks.

"Never mind her," Cidal replies. "How much did you hear?"

"Practically all of it."

"You have good ears. Your windows are rolled up."

"Well, it's hard to block out someone speaking so loudly."

"I see what you're saying."

From leaving the apartment complex to arriving at the estate of Lady Ila, the chauffer at different intervals throughout the trip glances suspiciously at Cidal in his rearview mirror. Cidal can feel the occasional glares from the driver without looking at him directly. He pretends that he doesn't notice. Not one single word is uttered.

As usual, Lady Ila greets him as he enters the house. Hugs and kisses which goes beyond good acquaintance.

"I missed you a whole lot, darling," she says.

"I missed you, too." He feels this is an appropriate response considering the circumstance.

"Come." She takes him by the hand to lead him to the terrace. "You must be starved."

"Well, all that I've had today is an apple."

"Really? Then you must be famished."

"I guess you can say that."

They enter the terrace. Everything is set. Plates, dishes, glasses. The food is kept warm under platters. They sit and enjoy good food and company. She informs him of her change in plans.

"I hope you don't mind, darling. We're heading out this evening instead of in the morning."

"Oh, yeah? What brought this on?"

"Nothing. I feel better this way. It doesn't get completely dark until late. It will be a nice evening ride."

"Okay. Sounds good to me."

After packing up once dinner was finished, they loaded the two-seat convertible. She lets him drive. With the top down, on a long stretch in the road, they drive on an evening spree.

27

She is always in the habit of rising before him. She loves getting early starts in the youngest part of the day while he sleeps until mid-morning, sometimes later. The cracking of sizzling eggs signifies the fresh new dew of dawn. Before reaching the horizon, the sun yawns and hesitates to get the first peek at the coming of day. The day will never exist without its presence.

The aroma of fresh cooking breakfast awakens his senses. A quick wash-up and a renewing of his body bring him into the kitchen where he finds Lady Ila adding the final touches to the first day meal.

"Good morning," he greets.

"Oh," she says as she turns to him. "Good morning to you too, sweetie. Breakfast is done."

"You have good timing," he tells her. He sits at the table.

"I'm beginning to know you a little too well. I seem to have picked up on how you schedule your day. That may be good. That may be bad. It all depends on how you look at it."

"Anything you do can't be all that bad."

She serves them both a traditional breakfast of scrambled

eggs, strawberry jam on rye toast, link sausages, and orange juice. She sits. They begin to eat.

"Mmm…it's good," he compliments her.

"No big deal. It's hard to ruin a simple meal."

"This is quite a place you have here. Way out of the way. In the country. Very nice and simple. But it has a very modest elegance about it too. How long have you had this place?"

"For many years. My late husband and I used to come here on rare occasions. Whenever we needed to get away from life in the city."

"Ahhh…so his spirit still lingers here."

For a brief moment, she closes her eyes and shakes her head. "Darling, don't. Don't even go there. That's all part of the past. A very good past. My concern is in the present."

"So what concerns you about the present?"

"It all depends on you."

"Me? Really? I never thought that you could ever give anyone that much power. Especially to someone like me."

"You underestimate yourself again. And you overestimate me. Why do you do this?"

"You seem to have a lot of influence. And plus, you have the money to do it."

"Uh-huh, I see. You mean the influence I have in art society. I know a good thing when I see it. It's not hard to convince others of like-mindedness to share the same viewpoints. I really haven't done anything."

"Am I as talented as I'm made out to be?"

"You're very mysterious. I can't quite figure you out yet.

That's exciting to me. I want to discover the clockwork that ticks inside of you."

"I'm just as curious about you too. Look what's happened between us since we first met. I never would've expected any of this. But I'm glad it happened."

"Sometimes things are done for selfish reasons. Other times things are done for the mutual of all who's involved."

"I don't follow you."

"It all goes back to favors, darling. I don't invest without a return on my investment. I believe I mentioned this once before."

Cidal does not say anything. He leaves his mind to wonder.

"Never mind that," she says. "We should enjoy our private time this weekend."

This is the sole purpose of the getaway. To clear the mind of clutter. To refresh the soul with nature's own ingredients of spirituality. And to free the body from the enclosed proximity of town life.

Plans are not in the abundance. There is nothing to be impressed with or to impress. If she really wanted to fascinate his senses, she would have taken a much different approach. She would have bypassed intimate inclusion for exotic places to wow his imagination. This is not her agenda. She wants from him, relaxation and restoration of all the hard work he has put forth. Still puzzled about who he is and the desire of finding the right key to open up the locked chest that holds all of his revelations, this gives her a chance to pick and probe.

Evening quiet times curling on a couch with there is moonlight and candles bringing intimacy to whispering conversations. By daylight, long walks in dense or open terrain, inhaling the freshness of clean natural air. Regardless of the surroundings, she tries her best to feel him out. He only tells her so much and leaves her guessing the rest. At times, she catches him scribbling a draft of his next project with pencil and paper. She is amazed of out quickly he comes up with images and ideas.

Late afternoon as they are walking back to the cottage, she decides to test his dedication to her, if any.

"Where are we?" she asks, leaving it for him to fill in the vagueness of the question.

As though he can sense what's on her mind, he answers. "Wherever you want us to be."

"Why, that's a very open-ended statement. I can take that wherever I want."

"Yes you can. And I believe you will. It's really not my decision, isn't it?"

"Well, of course it is, darling. It's not a one-way street. Decisions we make will be on a mutual agreement. I don't always call the shots."

"But you do have a lot of pull."

"Yes, in certain circles, I do. But that's business. I'm lucky to have the resources to obtain whatever I desire. However, whatever I desire is not always made of flesh and emotions. Meaning, most of the things I can attain are material. Our society places more importance on the market than what's personal. Finance has its place. But it isn't everything. One cannot hold tenderly or make love to a luxurious house, fancy car, and a bank account. It takes human connection to form a true bond that money cannot buy."

There is silence. A lingering, but non-agitated silence. A thoughtful engaging moment rather than the lack of words.

"Have you thought about my offer?" she asks. "The one I presented to you before."

"Oh! The one about living with you," he remembers. "I haven't decided yet."

"I know you haven't. And I don't believe you will."

"Why do you say that?"

"Do I have to tell you? You're a bright guy. You already know that you won't, but you don't know how to tell me. If you do it, you figure you owe me this favor, because of what you believe I've done for you. If that's your case, then I don't want it. It's not sincere enough."

"You're very upfront and logical. I like that."

"And yet I'm a woman too. Dealing with men, I have to be more logical than emotional when it comes to making a big decision. Which I don't believe it's big at all."

Cidal thinks for a moment. He remembers what Ms. Pearly said to him before leaving for the weekend.

"Will my art suffer from my decision?" he asks.

Lady Ila stops in her tracks. Cidal takes a couple more steps, stops, and looks back at her. She refuses to ask him what he means by this. Deep in her heart, there is an inference of her knowing. She begins walking again. Two steps past him, he catches up and continues to walk with her.

"You are a bright guy, aren't you?" she says without an inkling of emotion. She is calm and cool as she's always is. Very sure of herself.

He does not know how to take it. So he releases it into thin air.

Talk is only talk. There may be a meaning between the lines. What is not said can be more important than what is actually expressed. This does not seem to be a concern on either part. They immerse themselves through the rest of the day and into the intimate evening where their passion ignites. Pillow whispers captivate their sensuous connection. The moment is too engaging for there to be any disunity.

"I love making love to you," she says barely above a whisper. "I love how you make me feel. We fit very well…passionately."

"I feel the same way. You're a very vibrant woman in your sexually. I like that. You leave no can unopened."

"Is there anything you want to share with me?"

"Like what?"

She slightly chuckles. "Who you really are?"

"I'm no big deal. What you see is what you get."

"She chuckles again. "I hardly think so, darling. You have many mysteries. Tell me what they are."

"Well, first, I'm a very depressed individual. Severe depression I think they call it. Insanity. Suicidal thoughts. Suicidal actions. Real morbid stuff, you see. I'm walking down the middle of the road not knowing if I should lean over against the traffic or lean the other way and go with the flow of it. Not a ticking time bomb. I'm an explosion that has already occurred. Picking up the pieces not to reassemble the parts, but to throw them away. This is my story. This is my reality."

She remains quiet. Soaking in, absorbing what she's heard. Eventually, the mood hits her to lean over to plant a kiss on his lips. She lies back in her previous position.

"You've been holding out on me," she says, very softly. "You have another talent. Fictional writer."

28

After a long weekend of intimate excursions, the convertible pulls into the apartment complex mid-morning Monday. Ms. Pearly, who is always keen on what's going and coming, peeks out of her ground floor window where she sits. She tries her best to be inconspicuous. Cidal gets out of the driver's side of the car. Lady Ila leaves the passenger's side. The trunk pops open to retrieve his duffel bag. They share an embrace and a slight kiss on the cheek simultaneously. She gets behind the wheel, waves, and zooms out. Cidal walks towards the building. The closer he gets, a voice rings out.

"Didn't I tell you?"

He turns to the window and sees Ms. Pearly glaring at him.

"Hi. I guess you can see I'm back."

"Uh-huh. The gigolo. You're under her control now. How much is she paying you?"

"Nothing. What I earn is from my artwork."

"Ha!" She slams the window shut and goes about her business.

Cidal grins to himself, walks into the building, goes up the stairs, and into his apartment. He tosses his bag onto the floor of his bedroom to be dealt with later. He stirs around a bit, sends a

WeChat message to Wei Mei, and does the same with Yuli from China Romance Select before dabbling into his painting.

It is late Monday in China, so there is no expectation of a return message from Yuli. She must have or at least she should be in bed sleeping. Within the hour, Wei Mei connects with him. Not once did she ever try to contact him during the weekend. He is grateful for that. Circumstances would have prevented him from responding to her the way he would have liked to. Lady Ila was constantly around the whole time. Her curiosity may have titled her off-centered if she knew he was communicating with another woman. Unable to read her completely, Cidal did not want to be put in that situation to find out.

In their corresponding, Cidal lets Wei Mei know he will make arrangements to visit New York this upcoming weekend. Again, he apologizes for the sudden change of plans that derailed his previous schedule. She sits on the edge of the bed in her hotel room viewing the message. She has to convert the English into Mandarin with a press hold of the text. She sends a message back in Mandarin that he has to convert into English.

Very happy

She gets a phone call. She answers speaking Chinese. It lasts for only 30 seconds. Once again she sends a message back to Cidal.

Have visitors. I go now.

He realizes that she has clients waiting to see her. He responds.

Ok. Chat later.

There is a knock on her door. Wei Mei tidies herself up, walks over to the door, and peeks through the peephole. A typical westerner who has a fetish for Asian women awaits her. She waits a few seconds before opening the door to intensify his anxiety. She opens, they greet. He enters the room; the door closes. He tries his best to be hospitable, attempting to speak a little Chinese to her. With only a smirk on her face, she allows him to suffer through.

The hours of lunchtime rolls around. Lady Ila is sitting in a fancy restaurant at a booth table. One minute later, a woman of the same age and complexion and probably the same ethnicity, whatever that is, walks up to the table.

"I hope you weren't waiting long, she says."

"Hi, Marsay," Lady Ila greets. "No, as a matter of fact I just arrived."

Marsay sits down. A waiter comes to take their order.

"Give me a moment, please," Marsay says. "I want to see what you have on the menu first."

"All right, ma'am, take your time," the waiter says. "I'll be back shortly."

When he is out of earshot range, Marsay cannot wait to get all the information she can. But Lady Ila throws out the first compliment.

"Marsay, you're looking quite well."

"Oh, never mind that," she says, blowing it off. "Give me the details about this weekend with you and that artist of yours. I can't wait to hear."

Lady Ila laughs a little. "Nothing spectacular happened."

"Oh, c'mon! I don't believe that for a second."

"Really. We enjoyed our moments very quietly for the whole time we were there."

"How did you get him to come with you?"

"Quite simply. I told him that he needed the time off. To refresh and restore himself. At first, he mentioned other plans, but I got him to squash whatever they were. He seemed to really want to go…to come with me. There were no problems."

"So, Ila. That can't be all there is. I know the sex between the two of you is great from what you've told me before. But did you get anywhere else with him? You know. Some type of commitment?"

"Well, Marsay, I'll have to feel him out. He's hard to figure out at times."

"And you mentioned to me before that he doesn't want to move in with you."

"It's not that completely. I believe he feels he'll lose some independence if he did. He has his routine in the cubbyhole that he lives in. Which by the way is quite quaint. Very simple and modest. Just like him. Well, at least the modest part. He's a little bit more complicated than being just simple."

"What will you do with him?"

"I haven't a clue. Not yet."

"No, Ila! You? Don't know what to do? That's a first. I haven't seen you in this situation before."

"Relax, girlfriend. It isn't all of that. He doesn't consume my every thought like some childish schoolgirl. I'm at the stage in life where I'm very happy being who I am. If I choose to find a fella to ride the waves with, fine. If I don't, I know who I am. I'm okay with that also."

"He seems to be talented. You invited me to the art gallery to check out his work and to give my approval of him. I have to admit I do like his work."

"That's something else to discuss."

"What do you mean by that? You do think he's talented, don't you? You said so yourself once."

"Yes I did. I know…the art world is funny. You pull certain strings to get someone noticed. Influence. Money. So on and so forth. Then you pull other strings to retract what was set up."

"Uh-huh. I see what you're driving at. So, you, Ila…Lady Ila…can undo what you have already staged."

"Oh, honey!" she says sarcastically. "It really isn't up to me. It's up to him and how he acts."

They laugh. The waiter comes back to take their order.

While Cidal is being talked about, his ears aren't burning from the conversation. He continues to paint, stopping here and there for breaks, getting a bite to eat or leaving the compounds of enclosure to venture the outdoors.

Ms. Pearly is out on the grounds of the complex. Others are either coming or going; a few stay stranded for socializing. She spots him leaving and flings him her assumption.

"You going back to that woman, huh? You'll be a good artist as long as you stay with her. As soon as you pull out of her, she'll pull the rug out from under you, leaving you right back where you started. A poor struggling, scribbling, splash painter."

Cidal only acknowledges her with a slight nod, and no smile.

"Uh-huh. Ain't saying nothing, because you know it's true. Test her and see where you get."

He hops on his motor scooter, heading towards any destination. Where he's going is not the main focus. Fresh wind blowing to enliven a creative breeze.

On his journey to nowhere, something shakes him from inside. In spite of his artistic attainment, there is still something lingering in the backdrop of his outer facade. His mental instability races against an agitated spirit. Pouring deeper and deeper within him, a slow rising tide of confusion, strife, and uncertainty taints any hint of recent success. He fights against this onslaught by reminding himself that this particular phase of his life is over. He is now on a new stage. He is better equipped to handle the dogma of past blunders by the rejuvenating opportunities in career, financial status, and a strong possibility of finding a true relationship. But this is not enough to sustain him. He picks up speed in order to outrun, to escape his inner doings. Along the way, he hears a siren. He looks into his mirror of his handlebars and realizes he is being chased by law enforcement on a motorcycle. Eventually, Cidal slows down and pulls over to the side of the street.

The officer gets off the bike and gradually approaches Cidal. She is a woman of color of medium height and weight, wearing sunglasses.

"I don't have to tell you what you were doing," she says to him. "Where are you going in such a rush?"

"Sorry, Miss...I was just..."

"Let me see your driver's license," she interrupts. She isn't in any mood for small talk.

Cidal takes it out and hands it to her. She checks it out. "I'll be right back."

She goes back to her patrol bike and runs the information through. Cidal waits patiently, still struggling from within of the very thing he was attempting to escape from before being stopped. He mumbles to himself. Sentence structure and words are very incoherent. The officer does not hear or notice him going on to himself. By the time she receives what she needs, she walks back to Cidal. He is no longer mumbling.

"Your record is clean," she says, "but I'll have to give you this ticket." She hands it to him.

"This is my first," he says.

"Well, I surely hope that this will be your last. The court date is printed on it. Show up and pay for it or appeal it. The only thing I would not advise you to do is to skip out."

"I'll be there. Will you?" He says this in a way that doesn't take much imagination of the undertone flirtatiousness sprinkled on.

"I can be there right now to put you behind bars," she replies. "Which do you prefer?"

"I'll pay the ticket when the time comes."

Without another word, she walks back to her motorcycle. Cidal revs up his motor scooter and takes off.

Receiving a traffic ticket does nothing to soothe his aggravation. He mopes as he rides until finding himself driving into the parking lot of Dr. Madglove's office. He feels his soul expanding beyond the perimeter of his body. Talking to himself is no more a lone option. Someone else has to hear him out. He gets off his bike and walks in.

"May I help you, sir?" a receptionist of African descent asks when he approaches.

"Is Dr. Madglove in? I need to see him."

"Do you have an appointment scheduled?"

"No, but I've seen him a few times before."

"I'm sorry. You cannot see him without an appointment. And besides, he's out of the office for the next two days. I can schedule an appointment for you."

The receptionist searches her computer to check for the nearest available date to fit him in.

"What is your name, sir?"

"Cidal…Cidal Sewell."

"The earliest time I can get you in is next week at…"

"Next week?" he interrupts. "Are there that many crackpots walking around? Never mind. I'll be dead by that time." He turns and walks away.

The receptionist stands. "Obviously, you're in the wrong place, sir. The Rising Falls Emergency Ward is four blocks away."

As soon as Cidal is outside, he says to himself, 'Great! She's even a comedienne.'

In a distress mood, he wastes no time getting back home. Thank goodness Ms. Pearly is not around to inflict insult. He shuts the door behind him, goes to his bedroom, and collapses on the bed face down.

29

It seems the routine is starting all over again. Cidal wakes up and scratches a 5 o'clock shadow that now stands around 8 o'clock. It's about nightfall. He shoots a glance at the night-stand clock. 10:42. He gets up and refreshes himself. He walks into the kitchen; his stomach is ravaging for food. Being asleep for several hours is fine, he thinks, so he shouldn't be this hungry. He finds some leftovers in the fridge and sits at the table to satisfy his grizzly craving. A thought comes to him. He forgot to check his phone. Leaving the table for a swift return, he goes back into the bedroom, grabs his phone, and sits back down at the kitchen table to continue his meal.

He swipes the screen of his mobile open to see that he has seven missed calls and five unanswered messages. All the calls are from the same person. Lady Ila.

'Wow! That many?' Thinking aloud. 'I wonder what's up. We saw each other earlier this morning coming back from our weekend outing.' The clock on the kitchen wall stares at him. 11:13. 'It's too late to call now. I'm sure she's retired for the night. I'll call in the morning.' He finishes his leftovers and cleans up. Walking into the next room, he analyzes his current

216

portrait. His phone rings. He goes and retrieves it from the kitchen table. Flashes across the screen: Lady Ila. He connects immediately.

"Hi, Lady."

She sits comfortably on the side of her bed in a three-quarter length nightgown. "So you decide to come out of your shell of creativity to answer my call."

"Yes. Sorry about that. I fell asleep. Just woke up about a half-hour ago."

"Really? Lame excuse."

"No, I really did fall asleep. After you dropped me off this morning, I fiddled around a bit, left my apartment, came back, and collapsed. I've been sleeping for a few hours. I saw that I missed your calls. I was going to phone you in the morning, because of the late hour."

"You have no idea what's going on. Have you been drinking?"

"No. Just sleeping. What's going on?"

"I didn't drop you off this morning. That was two mornings ago."

"What! This is Monday night?"

"No, it's Wednesday night. I've tried to reach you for the last two days. You couldn't have been sleeping all that time."

Cidal shakes his head and rubs his eyes in disbelief. "It's starting all over again. I'm sorry, Lady. I'm not drunk. I honestly slept through the last couple of days? This isn't the first time it's happened. Periodically, I misplace days. I don't know if I'm coming or going. I think I'm in one day, but it's like I've been strategically picked up from one day and placed into another without knowing why."

"Oh, darling! That's sounds terrible. Maybe you need medical examination."

He doesn't want to explain the real cause, if indeed if it is the real cause of days converging into one or another. Reminding himself of Mother Goddess, and what she said about him walking a line between two existences. Cidal figures that Lady Ila would never believe such nonsense, so all he can do is to dismiss it.

"No, it's nothing. I feel fine. I'm sorry to put any worry on you. Did you try to come over when you couldn't get a hold of me?"

"No. I wanted to give you your space. I assumed you were overindulging yourself in your art, since you've been away from it the whole weekend."

"Yeah, I guess I'll be doing that up until this weekend."

"This weekend?"

"Oh, yeah, I'm getting confused again. For the rest of the week until the weekend."

"We need to go on another excursion."

"Oh, that would be nice. When?"

"I'll have to plan it out. You'll see. Well, darling, I have to get some rest. You know I'm more of a morning person. We'll talk soon. Goodnight."

"Okay. Goodnight."

Lady Ila continues to sit on the side of the bed contemplating. Her analytical mind tells her that he is keeping something from her that he doesn't want her to know about. And yet she realizes that she is in a better position than he is. He needs her to succeed and not the other way around. She feels confident that circumstances lie in her favor. She turns in for a peaceful sleep.

On the other hand, Cidal does not want to put Lady Ila on alarm about his condition of being absent from this world, being gone from reality without any recollection of what took place. In his mind, there is no way she can even begin to understand his inner dealings, his struggles of tug-of-war from within. However, this is a concern for him alone. Without being in a drunken state, he has no control over the unknown invisible phantoms lurking inside each crevice of his subconscious. Now that his life's activities are making an upward turn, he is becoming more aware that his predestined steps are following the footprints of another existence.

All night long he loses himself in his painting. Taking short breaks along the way. Sitting. Reflecting. Trying to make sense of his art, of his own life and where it is leading to. He leaves the apartment in the middle of the night to explore the secrets of natural darkness to grasp hold of something, anything that does not make sense so it can make sense to him. He slowly walks the empty streets with his hands in the front pockets of his pants. He wants to connect to whatever it is that needs to reveal itself to him. He checks his watch. He can barely see the exact time. He slips his mobile phone out of his pocket and swipes the screen. 3:13. Back it goes into his pocket.

Outside the center of town, in a dense wooded area, high in a tree sets a house. Not large. Not small. The cabin size is enough for a one large and two smaller rooms with indoor lighting. A rickety plank roped on both sides stretches from the house to another large connecting tree that has stepping stairs carved out from its huge trunk.

Blue Beans lurks out of his treehouse and walks onto his boarded porch. He examines the darkness around his private haven and perks his ears to hear what he cannot see like an animal in the wild keeping its senses keen on any imminent danger. A clear bright moon shines above. He sits on the edge of his porch with his legs dangling, swinging his feet. That typical characteristic of a half-crazed smirk crosses his face.

Sitting on a bench in the middle of town, Cidal tries to collect his thoughts by allowing the fresh night air to fuel his imagination. Very few drivers pass by in vehicles. A pedestrian here. Two or three there. There always seem to be someone in the streets at all hours of day or night.

To his surprise, a dink comes through his mobile. And by the sound of it, he knows it's a WeChat signal. He takes out his phone to check. There is a message. He goes into the app to find the message was sent by Yuli from China Romance Select.

'Why is she up so late?' he asks himself. Then it dawns on him. She is twelve hours ahead of his time. It's going on 3:30 am in Rising Falls, but it's already close to 3:30 pm in the afternoon in China.

She asks him what he is looking for in a wife. After he translates it from Chinese characters to English, he thinks for a moment. Then he shoots out a response.

I'm looking to share my life with someone.

Yuli is quite surprised to get such a quick response. Out of curiosity, she sends another message.

> *You up? Why?*
> *Slept all day. Up painting.*
> *Oh. I see. Why have you no married?*
> *Waiting for the right one.*
> *Not good answer. At 20's. At 30's. Maybe. Not at 45 years old.*
> *I was trying to make something of myself before asking a woman to marry me. I'm getting there now.*
> *Also not good answer. Do you love the God?*
> *Yes, I love God.*
> *Oh, so you Christian?*
> *Not really.*
> *What you mean?*
> *I don't practice any organized religion.*
> *Nonsense. How can you love the God? Only Christian.*
> *Christians don't have sole ownership on God.*
> *Bible say not this. Bible is true. You are false.*
> *I'm open-minded to all religions without practicing one.*
> *You are dishonest person. Liar you not be Christian.*
> *I don't want to get into this religion thing.*
> *Why? My future husband Christian. No sinner.*
> *I have not been dishonest. I speak truth.*
> *Wrong! You not talk Bible, you speak liar's tongue. You not Christian, you don't love the God.*

*I would be a very good husband. I would give my wife
lots of love. Faithful and dedicated to her every need.*

*Your love will fail with no Christian love. No love of God, no
love of wife. Again, you talk no real truth of the God. You speak
from yourself. This is arrogance. Only the God knows. You know
nothing of the God. I want nothing of this selfish love.*

But I would love my wife endlessly.
*Why do you argue with me! You make so angry! You no
Christian! You cheat!*

Cidal apologizes for the misunderstanding of their con-versation. But to no avail. She does not answer his message. He was not prepared to experience this sort of jostling in the middle of his night. It doesn't take a mind full of wisdom for him to come to the conclusion that this match will not work for either of them. So he sits there, thinking about the transaction that took place. Because of his interaction with Yuli, he does not notice a figure sitting across the street with fixed eyes on him. Blue Beans glares at him. By turning his head to take in the surroundings of where he is, only then does Cidal realizes that he is being watched. A slight grin and a nod of the head come from Blue Beans.

'Great,' Cidal says under his breath. 'Does this guy ever sleep?'

Cidal keeps fidgeting with his phone to keep his focus off of him. The longer he goes without looking in his direction, the better chance that Blue Beans will get up and go about his business. He does this, trying to keep him in his peripheral vi-sion, so he will know when he leaves. Time ticks by. It doesn't happen. 4:00 turns into 4:15. By this time, Cidal is fed up and makes his move. He stands to walk away, shooting a gander in his vicinity. Blue Beans has not moved a muscle.

"Hey, friend!" Blue Beans shouts, throwing his hand up signifying a wave.

"Hey!" Cidal returns the greeting.

"Nice night to be out, isn't it?"

"Yes it is."

"You're a night creeper. Just like me."

"Oh, okay." Cidal doesn't want to say too much so he can be on his way back home.

"Leaving so soon, my friend?"

"Yeah. Gotta get back home."

"I'll see you around. You know me."

"Yeah, sure. Don't I know it."

Continuing on his journey home, he checks his phone periodically to see if Yuli has returned his last message. She hasn't. This may be the last of their corresponding. He quickly forgets the bizarre encounter. Until he is home, his mind searches for ideas to complete his unfinished work. He arrives back to his apartment and paints into the wee hours of the morning.

30

A thought weighs heavily on Cidal's mind. He does not want to rock the boat. Equally, he does not want to be caught standing on a sinking ship. Being aware that he cannot have it both ways, he chooses the bold approach. If the boat rocks, then let it.

He texts Lady Ila.

Wearing sweat outfits, Lady Ila and her friend Marsay are strolling through the park after a nice powerwalk exercise. This is something they do twice a week, depending on their schedules. The conversation is light. A word or two here or there. A signal goes off.

"Oh, is that my phone or yours?" Marsay asks as they both check their pockets.

Looking at her screen, "It's mine," Lady Ila says. She stops momentarily to read the content.

"Anything wrong?" Marsay asks.

After reading the text, Lady Ila has an expression of deep thought. "No," she says. "Just his timing." They begin to walk again.

"Oh, your lover artist. What's he up to? Or am I getting too personal?"

"Marsay, you know I share everything with you. He's going to New York this weekend."

"Oh, is he? Uh-huh."

"Don't give me that 'uh-huh' business," Lady Ila says with a grin. "It means nothing."

"Do you really believe that?"

"Of course I do. He's not chained to me."

"But you do have him on a leash, ready to pull back at any given moment."

"No."

"Maybe it's a long leash, but it's still a leash."

"I hold no burden on him. He's free to do whatever he wants."

Marsay laughs. "You don't believe that for a second. I know you all too well. Are you going to text him back?"

"I'll have to think about what I want to say first."

"Did he say how he was going? Alone or with a friend?"

"Believe me. I'll find out."

"When did he say he was leaving?"

"Later this evening."

"Is this a spur of the moment decision or did he have this planned?"

"I really can't tell you."

"So you didn't know anything about it prior to the text."

"Nothing." A sudden thought comes to Lady Ila. "Wait! He did mention something about having plans last weekend when I wanted to take him to my country cottage. He didn't specify what they were though. And I didn't ask him either. I'm wondering now is he picking up this weekend what he dropped last weekend."

"And he didn't say what those plans were? Not even a hint?"

"No, he didn't."

"Yes, girlfriend. You better check into this. But then again it could be nothing. You better find out for sure."

"Don't worry. I intend to."

Cidal is gathering last minute items at a store for his New York trip. The basics are toiletries of day-to-day. Tooth paste, mouthwash, deodorant, shaving cream and after shave lotion, and other amenities. He walks out of the store and goes to an ATM machine to withdraw x amount of dollars. His flight departs at 6:15 pm. Getting to the airport two hours before takeoff is an idea time, because of security reasons or any other holdups for that matter. According to his watch, it is 12:35. It may be time-consuming to slip in a meal later before the trip, so he ventures the streets undecided on what to eat. His phone rings. Lady Ila is displayed on the screen. He answers.

"Hey Lady! You get my text?"

"I sure did."

She sits in her convertible with the top down, wearing sunglasses at the apartment complex of where Cidal lives. Ms. Pearly is peeping out of her window, keeping close tabs on what is happening around the premise.

"I'm out buying a couple of things for the trip. Don't want to be caught short of anything. Where're you at?"

"At your place. I thought I would come by to see you before you leave. What time does your flight depart?"

"Oh, really? 6:15."

"Where exactly are you?"

"In the middle of town. At the intersection of Crossnut and Junebug."

"That's not far at all."

"I'll be there in a few."

"Okay. I'll wait here."

Ms. Pearly has a clear view of Lady Ila. 'Uh-huh. I wonder what she waiting on?' she says to herself. Her curiosity keeps her hawkish eyes piercing in her direction. The last thing she wants to do is to miss something significant. In a matter of moments, Cidal shows up on his motor scooter. He gets off. He carries a couple of small bags of items he bought. Lady Ila sees him and gets out of her car. Cidal spots her right away and makes his move towards her. They meet and greet.

"I hope I wasn't too long," Cidal says.

"No, you weren't. You had no idea I was coming."

"Let's go in."

They start walking towards the building. Cidal glances over to the window where Ms. Pearly stays. He doesn't see her. As soon as they step to the door, a voice comes from Ms. Pearly's window.

"Uh-huh!"

Still, he doesn't see her when he quickly shoots a glance in that direction. He opens the door for the two of them and they walk in and up.

The door closes of his upstairs apartment. No words are said. Cidal puts the bags on the kitchen counter. Conversation begins.

"So why New York all of a sudden?" she asks.

"I had it planned already," he replies.

"How long ago was this in the making?"

"In a matter of days."

"And so these past two days when you were out of it, in another world dosing off, you had enough wherewithal to schedule a New York trip. I see."

"Exactly I had to rearrange my schedule from last week to this week."

"The weekend we were gone was the same weekend you had other plans?"

"Yes."

"Why did you tell me this trip was so important? I would've understood and rescheduled our outing for another time."

"I really wanted to spend the weekend with you."

"That's sweet of you, darling. You don't have to flatter me. I assumed you were doing something around town, so that's why I asked you to break it. It would've been nice to know. Don't feel that you can't tell me anything."

"I owed it to you, to us, to take that trip. Nothing was lost."

"Okay, darling."

The slight distance between them closed. They embrace. They kiss. He takes her by the hand and escorts her to the couch. His arm is around her shoulders as they sit close. He nibbles a little on her ear. She allows him, but her subtle expression indicates there is more on her mind. She owes it to herself, to her image, that she will never allow herself to play the role of a desperate woman. Worst yet, a middle-aged desperate woman. She knows she has too much influence and resources to bow down to any silly schoolgirl behavior. She holds the power. The cards are in her hands. In her echoing mind, she reminds herself of this.

As he continues to be flirtatious, he senses that she is not in the mood for playfulness. However, her poise, her coolness of a cucumber, she allows him the enjoyment of sensuality. Since it seems she is not taking any initiative of their familiar encounter, Cidal wants to be sure the status of consent is agreeable to her.

"Anything wrong?" he asks.

"No, I'm perfectly fine," she replies with a grin of neither approval nor disapproval.

His perception is too keen not to go forth without willing participation. So he stops, takes his arm from around her; continuing to sit close while holding her hand.

"Why did you stop?" she asks.

"Forcing a liaison has never been my thing. It has to come naturally and mutually."

"I haven't stopped you."

"Yes, you have. The timing is bad I'm sure."

"How are you getting to the airport?"

"Taxi."

"What time do you want to be there?"

"Around 4:15."

"I can take you if you want."

"Good. Since you're here, I was hoping you'd offer. I appreciate it."

"You don't have to mention it. It's nothing."

"Thanks just the same. You've done so much for me."

"And vice-versa. We've both benefited. It's give-and-take. Open-and-share is what I prefer to call it."

"Well, I'm grateful for everything you'd shared with me."

"And I appreciate your openness."

Because of the sudden change in climate, Cidal does not know if he should test the waters again to see if the mood is there. His intuition tells him that she is too clever to allow herself to succumb to intimate advances over a few kind words. This does not give him the green light to go forth. But at the same time, he does not want to deny her if she is willing, however subtle she is about it.

"Where do we go from here?" he asks. His stomach growls.

"You must be hungry."

"Yes I am. I could also use some food."

She is keen on his innuendo. She allows it to happen. "Okay. Dessert first, then we can leave to have a late lunch before dropping you off at the airport."

From then on, there is no dialogue. Just action. He leads her quietly by the hand into the bedroom.

31

Lady Ila drives up to the Southwest Airlines departure terminal where luggage can be checked in from the outside. Cidal leans over and plants a kiss on her lips.

"Thanks for the ride."

"You're much welcome. Let me know when you land in New York."

"Okay."

He gets out of the convertible; she pops open the trunk with a push of a button by the steering wheel. He retrieves his baggage, his laptop in its carrying case, and closes the trunk. She blows him a goodbye kiss and heads out. After checking in his luggage, he walks into the airport and directs his steps towards security that would lead him to the proper gate with his laptop strapped over his shoulder. By glancing at his boarding pass, he looks at the time and which gate his plane will be taking off from. 6:15 is the time. The security line doesn't seem to be long on a Thursday evening. He notices that the line is going smoothly without any holdups. In a breeze he is through. Gate A-19 is his destination.

While sitting at the gate, there is a little more than an hour before flight takeoff. He sends a WeChat message to Wei Mei, asking her which hotel she is staying at. Within 35 minutes, she responds with the name and address. A smiley face accommodates the end of her message. Before too long, the call to board the aircraft is being announced. Cidal steps onboard and takes a window seat. Right on schedule at 6:15, the plane makes its way to the runway and streams the skies.

Cidal has never been to New York before. Around two hours of flying, the plane descends upon New York City. Getting off and heading towards the baggage claim area, Cidal texts Lady Ila to let her know that he got there safely. Her reply is quick. Telling him to enjoy his trip. He grabs his luggage and exits the airport building to find waiting cabs. He chooses one, climbs in, and lets the taxi driver know where he wants to go.

The cabdriver is full of conversation. He speaks with an accent which Cidal could hardly place. But he understands every word he says. The driver is off on his own tangent. Talking just to be talking. Going from one topic to another with barely two seconds of breath in-between. Weaving in and out of traffic, the driver steadily talks, keeping his eyes on the road and occasionally glances back at Cidal by turning his head instead of looking into the rearview mirror. All Cidal can do is nod in agreement by tossing in some 'yesses, uh-huh, and I see' to hold up his very short end of the one-sided conversation.

Twenty minutes later, they pull into a middle-end hotel. Cidal thanks him and gives him a healthy tip.

"Thanks brother for hearing me out and for the tip."

"Think nothing of it."

"Enjoy your stay in New York. I hope you like it."

"I believe I will. Thank you."

Cidal gets out with his luggage and laptop. He registers at the front desk. After the preliminaries of showing ID, paying, and signing forms, he is given a card key to room 211. He goes up the elevator and into the room, lays his suitcase on one of the two beds, kicks off his shoes, and sits on the side of the other bed. Taking out his phone, he sends a message to Wei Mei. As he waits for her to get back to him, he freshens up with a shower and a shave.

Wei Mei finishes business with one client. She escorts him to the door. He attempts to say goodbye in Chinese, but misses the mark. She smiles and says goodbye in English. She opens the door and closes it shortly after he steps out. There are also two beds in her room. A bed where she conducts her business of play, and the other for her own personal use for night sleeping. Her mobile phone is on her personal bed. She sits on it and makes a call to her boss, speaking Chinese, letting her boss know that her client has left.

It's after 9:00. She has no idea if she will be entertaining another client for the evening. She checks her WeChat messages. She perks up to see that Cidal is one of two to three people who have left her a message. She reads it and sends back a response.

His showering and shaving are complete. He slips into some other clothes while checking his phone. A green blinking light in the top left corner signifies a WeChat message. He sends out a response of his own. He mills around the room a little, killing time. He pops on the flat screen to see if anything catches his interest. As usual, nothing. Not even a good sporting event is playing. So he keeps it on for company.

Roughly around 10:10, 10:15, a gentle knock comes to his door. He cuts the television off, goes to the door, and looks through the peephole. There stands Wei Mei on the other side. Cidal opens immediately. They greet as she walks in. The door closes. There are hugs and kisses.

"I miss you," she says.

"I miss you, too," returning the compliment. "I glad you can get away."

"Is happy to see you."

"I'm happy to see you too. Are you done for today?"

"Yes. No visitors."

She takes the initiative to touch his face with the palm of her hand and strokes it.

"I've already shaved so no five o'clock shadow."

"No five o'clock. Almost half past ten."

He laughs.

"Why you laugh?" she asks.

"Oh, it's nothing. Just American slang."

They walk over to sit on the side of the bed. Closely. His arm is in back of her; his hand holding the other side of her posterior cheek. They share a short passionate kiss. A little of her lipstick smudges his lips. Very lightly, her forefinger rubs it in. He smiles.

"Now I have a piece of you with me."

"How long you stay?" she asks.

"Sunday evening I leave. You will be busy?"

"Maybe little busy. Friday and weekend busy."

"I want to spend some time with you."

"You come for me?"

"Yes."

"Okay. I will try not so busy."

"He chuckles a little. "Okay. Let's hope. Are you hungry?"

"No hungry. Little snack."

"Can you leave?"

"Yes."

"Will you get in trouble?"

"It's okay. No tell boss."

"Okay, let's go get ice cream."

"Okay. I call Xia."

Wei Mei calls and speaks in Chinese to her friend and co-worker to let her know where she is going and who she will be with. She ends the call. "Okay. All done."

On the way to the hotel earlier that evening by taxi, Cidal remembers passing by an ice cream parlor not far from where they're staying. He estimates the walk being a good 15 or 20 minutes away. By car, 6 or 7, maybe 8 at the most. After going down the elevator to the first floor, they leave the hotel and head through the parking lot and down the street.

It is a locally owned ice cream shop. Not a commercial brand name scattered across the country. They walk in to order, and then they take a seat at one of several tables provided outside. He has a large paper bowl container of mixed vanilla and chocolate fudge, and she has a small vanilla with lots of sprinkled charms. The night is perfect. A warm breeze accommodates the company of outside dwellers.

"Very nice we come here," she says.

"It's good to be here with you."

"I'm glad you like."

"Do you like it here in New York?"

"Yes I like. Xia like more. She like big city. You like?"

"What I see so far I like."

"What you do here?"

"I don't know yet. Main reason is you."

"Really?" She says this as though she had nothing to do with inviting him to come see her.

"Yes. No invite from you. No New York for me."

"Is very happy you come."

"I'll have to see you in spurts."

"Spurts?"

"Yeah. Here and there. I have to see you when you are free."

"I try. Will ask boss for day off."

"That would be good."

"Boss may say no."

"It doesn't hurt to ask. Do you get days off?"

"When first come to New York. One week."

"Really? One week off?"

"Yes. Very nice time."

"I see. You and Xia?"

"Yes. Two other girls."

"Uh-huh. That's nice you all stick together."

They continue to eat their ice cream without much talk. Enjoying present company, feeling the nice climatic environment. The hour is getting late. They finish up and start to make their slow motion pace back to the hotel. An idea pops into her mind.

"You go Chinatown with me?" she asks.

"Yeah, that would be good. When?"

"I ask boss for tomorrow evening off."

"Okay."

"Work all day. No work evening. We go Chinatown."

"If we can, let's do it."

"Okay. I let you know tomorrow."

They walk back into the hotel. "What room number are you?" he asks.

"Room number 1-1-2."

Cidal's watch ticks-tocks at 11:53. "Almost midnight. You better get some sleep."

"Yes. Up all day. I will sleep-uh. You rest too."

He drops her off at her door. A goodnight kiss and one last embrace before he goes back up to his room. But first he tells her:

"I will WeChat you in the morning," he says to her.

"Okay. Night night."

Already he has taken his shower before going out. Cidal puts on his pajamas and brushes his teeth. Surprisingly, when checking his phone, there isn't a text or call from Lady Ila. He figures she is letting him have his lay of the land, but ready to drop a call on him when he least expects it. Also to his surprise, his phone never went off once during the short time he was with Wei Mei. However, that would not have been a big deal to him. He was prepared to handle the situation if and when it arose, which it didn't.

Not feeling totally tired or sleepy, Cidal props himself up on top of the bed and cuts the TV on. Something he very seldom does at home. His artwork is not around for him to fiddle with. He could pop on the computer and search the net, but decides to just take it easy until restlessness creeps up and snatches him from behind. He flips through the stations by remote and stops at a sports channel. One of the most popular ones. ESPN. Within ten minutes of watching, the sound automatically goes off. He searches for the mute button, pressing it on and off, testing to see if that works. It doesn't. He cuts off the TV, waits for 15 seconds, and then cuts it back on. Picture is fine. Still no sound.

A soft voice calls out. *What will you do now?*

He looks around the room. There is nothing hiding. The glow from the television shines and the lamp by his bedside illuminates its brightness. Then it dawns on him. The voice is too familiar. Slowly materializing in a cushion comfort chair in the corner of the room, Mother Goddess appears.

"Oh, I thought it had to be you," he says. "You come to New York too, huh."

What will you do now? She repeats.

"I don't know. Maybe check the batteries in the remote."

There is nothing wrong with your vision box. What will you do with the situation you are currently in?

"I don't understand."

The girl here or the woman there?

"Oh, I gotcha. I don't know. Does it matter?"

No. Everything will take care of itself in the end. I'm curious on what decision you will make.

"You're in the spirit world, Mother Goddess. Should you already know?"

There are certain things in life that one cannot control. Your fate, for instance. But the things that one can control, dictates destiny. Regardless of what you do or don't do, it will be affected by it.

"So my results will be the same no matter what I do."

Maybe. I believe we traveled down this road before.

"How does she feel about me?"

You have two different hearts involved. Both are hard for you to read. The girl here comes from a culture where women do not express love or affection in the same way you would expect your culture to. The woman there, back in Rising Falls, is too sophisticated to allow her love to be seen by any man unless she is sure of his dedication.

"That's about sums it up. You're not going to tell me how it will go?"

You have already decided for yourself which way you will go.

"No matter how upbeat things are, I still feel I'm going south. My mind, the inside of me doesn't match what's happening to my outside life. My artwork has taken off for some strange reason. Thanks to you. Maybe I'm talented. Maybe I just got lucky on a whim. Whichever way, I don't feel it's enough to satisfy my heart, to settle my mind. I thought a little success would do it, but at times, it hasn't done a thing. It seems I'm running from myself and I can't catch up, leaving me frustrated with myself, with my life. Days are still misplaced. I even feel things that I can't explain or even see. I get this strong urge inside that things exist without physical evidence. Visions and different images creep into my brain. But not only that, there's this heavy connection between those things and me. Maybe my old manager was right. Depression leads to insanity or vice-versa."

He waits for her to respond. But she doesn't. Her thoughts seem to be millions of miles away. He can sense it. But they're not. What appears to be a disconnection between what he says and how she is reacting gives him a falsity of spiritual reality.

"No words?" he asks. "No comments?"

There is none.

"You will not give me any explanation?"

You have said it all and don't even realize it. All of your problems are solved by your questions. All of your questions are solved by your answers. Your spirit will be great in the world to come.

Mother Goddess looks at the television. The mute becomes sound again. *We didn't need any outside distractions. Now you can go back to enjoying your program.*

She disappears quicker than she appeared before.

After much time, slowly, his eyelids give into the heavy weight of rest until he is straddling between his conscious reality and deep sleep. In a haze of either or, his door opens and in walks Wei Mei. She closes the door behind her while still facing him. Gradually, she approaches his bed. Dressed in only her sensuous lingerie, she crawls onto the bed like a tigress about to surprise an unsuspecting prey. He watches her the whole time. The lighting in the room is very dim. Cidal is still leaning against the head board of the bed in the same position earlier, before drifting off. She crawls on top, straddles his body, and slowly disrobes. Mutually, passion gives into both desires. Not uncontrolled. But soothing. Not shallow. But deep-rooted and planted from another existence. A connection which goes beyond the physical. Their sexually becomes metaphysical. In tune with everything spiritual. It lasts as long as it is supposed to last. Then, total darkness eclipses him.

32

Early Friday morning, Cidal awakes and she is not there. The television is off. The remote placed neatly on the nightstand beside him. Nothing must have happened. It must have been all a dream. Physically, he can feel he is part of the room. Internally, he is somewhere else. Some unknown place. Two opposing streams converging into one heading out to sea.

He checks his phone to confirm it is Friday morning, and not some other morning, afternoon, or evening on another day. It matches up. Any messages from Wei Mei? WeChat indicates nothing new. He gets himself together performing the morning ritual of refreshing and a quick wash up. He changes into his clothes to go down for breakfast.

Breakfast is served every morning between the hours of 7 to 9. He enters the dining room around 8:30. Quite a few people are having breakfast or finishing up. He gets a plate and goes around the buffet to select varies breakfast foods. Never a real coffee drinker, but only on occasions, he chooses orange juice instead. There is an empty table in the corner that he spots and casually walks over to sit.

As he eats, he glances around the room, observing different patrons. A particular table comes to his immediate attention. In the center of the room, a table of four, Wei Mei sits with three other Chinese women, having their breakfast. She has kept close tabs on him since he entered the room, unbeknownst to him. She smiles without bringing any notice to herself. He lifts his glass of orange juice as a toast. She nods shyly and continues on with her company. Cidal eats and scans through his mobile phone which is lying on the table, ignoring Wei Mei and her circle of friends just to be obscure. Midway through completing his meal, he notices the table she and her friends were at sets unoccupied. A dining room worker collects plates, cups, and other utensils, and wipes down their table. He gets a WeChat message. It's Wei Mei.

Will be busy. Chat later.
He sends back a reply. *Okay.*

Cidal goes back up to his room after completing breakfast and brushes his teeth. For the first time in a long time, he has nothing to occupy his time. All of his artwork is back in Rising Falls. What to do? He ventures out and explores the sights.

Around 12:30, Lady Ila and her friend Marsay are having lunch at a quaint restaurant. The weather is perfect for an outside meal on the terrace. Tables are shaded by large umbrellas protruding out from the center. They shoot the breeze about everything under the sun until one person in particular is mentioned.

"So, what's going on with him?" Marsay asks. "What's the scoop with New York all of a sudden?"

"I haven't spoken to him since I left him at the airport," Lady Ila says. "He texted me once he got there safely."

"Since then, nothing?"

"It hasn't been 24 hours since we last communicated. This is Friday afternoon. I dropped him off Thursday evening. I'll give him some time. I don't want to become a bug-a-boo as they say."

"Did he ever say why he was going to New York?"

"No, and I didn't even ask him."

"Aren't you curious?"

"The thought has struck my mind. I'm not overwhelmed by it. If he really wanted me to know, he would've said so."

"Does he have relatives there?"

"He was an orphan."

"In that case, it only means one thing. And you know what that one thing is, don't you? I don't need to tell you."

"Maybe it is. Maybe it isn't."

"If it was me, I would get to the bottom of it. I would want to know what's going on."

"The keys are in my hands. Remember that. Everything that is accessible to him, I control. With this viewpoint, I'm not concerned about anything. If anyone should be walking on eggshells, it's him. Not me."

"So? Are you going to call and check up on him?"

"I'll call. But it wouldn't be to check up. I'll call to see how he's doing, and if he's enjoying New York. That's all."

"Well, I certainly hope you know what you're doing. You seem to have it under control."

Lady Ila chuckles. "I try to do my part."

A signal sounds from a mobile phone.

"That could be my phone," Lady Ila says. Taking her phone out of her purse, she sees that there is a text message. "It's him."

"Your lover artist?"

"Yes." She reads the single word from the text. *Hey!* She texts back her response. *Hey yourself!* With a smiley icon at the end.

"Anything new?" Marsay asks.

Lady Ila puts her phone back inside her purse. "Oh, no. Nothing new. He just wanted to say hey."

"Uh-huh. How sweet of him!" Marsay says sarcastically.

"Isn't it though? He's such a romantic charmer," Lady Ila responds, being just as sarcastic.

"This is his way of checking in with you probably."

"I don't hold him to anything. I just allow him to be. You do know how these artists are? It's their nature to be whatever."

"Well, in a very subtle way, you may have a 'whatever' on your hands."

"And if I do, darling, I know exactly how to handle him."

The comfort of being alone is quite welcoming for Cidal. Back home in Rising Falls or here in New York, his journey relies on his own footing. Always alone, never with any company, he takes his own tour by foot or bus. As usual, there is no rush to get to any particular place. He follows the stream of anticipation, letting the nature of everything take its course. Subways to taxis, going from one place to another, he observes people of different ethnicities and cultures, listens to varies languages of recent or well-established immigrants. Getting a bite to eat when on the run, he takes in a small restaurant. Eventually, he finds his way back to the hotel by taxi.

Without his art to keep him occupied or to sustain his creative mode, Cidal feels like a lost soul wandering about without purpose. He kicks off his shoes to get more comfortable before lying across the bed. Reaches for the remote on the nightstand and pops on the TV. His phone has not signaled a message of any kind since he last sent a very short text to Lady Ila. Nothing from Wei Mei. Yet. The exhaustion of early day, he drifts in and out of a light sleep.

Around 5:00 late afternoon, Wei Mei dwindles on her phone while sitting on the side of the bed in her hotel room. Her friend, Xia, is in the room with her, standing and pacing lightly. The conversation is quite involved, speaking their native tongue. Her friend has more to say than she does. After a few more moments of dialogue, Wei Mei gets up and throws her purse strap over her shoulders. They have a couple of last encouraging words before she leaves the room.

Cidal is still lying on the bed. He begins to toss-n-turn and decides it's time to get up. There's a knock on his door. Walking towards and standing at the door, he sees Wei Mei through the peephole. He opens and lets her in.

"Oh, wow. I wasn't expecting you," he tells her. They share a hug and a light kiss.

"I WeChat you. You no answer," she says.

They go over to the bed, and he picks up his phone and checks for missed messages. There are three WeChat messages from her that he hasn't read.

"Oh, I'm sorry. I drifted off a little."

"Drifted off?"

"Yes, I fell asleep watching TV."

"Okay. You sleep-uh well?"

"Just a catnap. The moments I was asleep, it was good."

"You tired?"

"No, not now. I'm fine."

"Want to go out?"

"Sure. Where to?"

"We go Chinatown. Remember?"

"Oh, yeah! That's right! Let me wash-up and get myself to-gether."

"Okay."

She sits on the bed while Cidal goes into the bathroom and tidies himself. He comes out and uses his phone to locate the closes bus stop that would take them to the east side of Man-hattan.

"There's a hop-on, hop-off bus stop not too far from here," he says.

"I happy you go."

"Are you kidding? It will be nice to be with you in China-town. I'm glad you asked. So I gather you're off for the rest of the day."

"Yes. No worries."

"It's okay with your boss, isn't it?"

"You no worry. Okay?"

"If you say so."

"I say."

Delight is taken in the sharing of her culture, or as much as she can without being in her own country. They are about to get ready to leave. Wei Mei mind comes to her like a sudden wave across her head.

"I almost forget it," she says. "I give you bonus last night. I come here. You don't pay. I give you bonus."

Cidal has to think for a second on what she means. Then he gets the revelation. "You came here last night to see me?"

"Yes, that's right. You lay on top of bed. I come in."

He begins to think to himself that the whole occurrence wasn't a dream. It was a reality which transfixed his mind into believing he was in another state of existence.

'It starting to happen again,' he says to himself, puzzled.

"What? What you say?"

"Oh, nothing. Just thinking out loud. Let's go."

Waiting at the nearest bus stop, it doesn't take long for a bus to come by. They board. She first and then he follows.

"Where to Mack?" the bus driver asks in a gruff voice.

"Manhattan's East Side. Chinatown."

"Okay." The driver closes the door. The two take a seat.

"Not long way," Wei Mei says to Cidal, sitting close to him.

"My mobile info says 30 minutes from here to there."

"You like Chinatown?"

"I've never been there. But I will like."

"So happy you like."

Scenic views of the city and surrounding areas as the bus carries a full load from Flushing to the east side of Manhattan. There the two get off and start exploring the sights, sounds, and smells of Chinatown. Mandarin is spoken at every turn. Chinese characters on signs and buildings. The aroma of Chinese food tantalizes taste buds for those who have a craving. Music can be heard coming from some unknown, unseen place. Bustling pedestrians; vehicles fill the streets.

"Wow, this makes me feel that I'm actually in China somewhere," Cidal says.

"You want to go?" Wei Mei asks. "China?"

"Yes. Someday I will get there."

"You come Shanghai. I show you."

"Can't wait."

"When you come?"

"I don't know. When do you go back?"

"I don't know."

"How long will you be in New York?"

"Boss will say."

"I hope you come back to Rising Falls."

"I want to come."

"Good. I can spend lots of time with you."

"When you go back?"

"Sunday evening."

"We can come Chinatown again."

"Yes, before I leave, that's good."

"Very happy. Okay."

They walk along to observe everything around them with swiveling heads and open eyes. Shops, stores, eateries, museums displaying the culture and history of the Chinese and Chinese-Americans. Large doses of Chinatown they absorb while making their own tour without the slanted perspective of western guides. As they take their time exploring, they step inside Shanghai Asian Manor for a bite of dinner. Time seems to be at a standstill. They make sure to savor every moment of togetherness surrounded by all that she is familiar with back home.

"I really like this place," Cidal says.

"Restaurant?" she asks.

"Oh, yes. The restaurant too. But all of Chinatown. If you're free tomorrow, let's do it again."

"I see about boss. Maybe."

Ordering food, waiting, and eventually digesting slowly their delicacies of Chinese cuisine, they engage in casual conversation. It dawns on him to ask or to get clarification of what was said early.

"Let me get this straight. You came to my room last night?"

She looks at him as though his brain is detached from his head. "You don't know memory?"

"Kind of. Kinda foggy. Not too clear."

"You forget me easy."

"No! I can never forget you. Lately, I don't know where I'm at sometimes. You left before the night was over."

To this she says nothing. Only---"You no pay."

"Oh! You want me to pay?" He reaches inside his pants pocket.

"No, no. Gift from me. No pay."

"Okay. What does this mean?"

"I like you. You no like?"

"Yes I do like. I like you very much."

"You look for girlfriend?"

"Maybe."

"Maybe?"

"You're right. You are my girlfriend now."

"Really? I like too. You boyfriend."

"15 years difference."

"15 years? So? Problem?"

"No, not for me. You're 30. I'm 45."

"You no look your age."

"Thank you. Sometimes it's hard to guess the age of Asian women."

"Oh! What to do?"

"What to do about what?"

"I still work…"

Cidal knows exactly where she's going with the conversation. He intervenes. "Don't worry. You can still work for your boss."

"I still see client?"

"Yes, for right now. Maybe later, we will see about it then. Right now, okay."

"You no like me with visitors?"

"Keep doing what you're doing. It's fine for now."

"Okay."

Through the course of their meal, Cidal receives two text messages. Both times he glances at his phone to see who it is from. Lady Ila. Her curiosity strikes her to know how and what he's doing. Especially on a Friday evening in a big town like New York. There are swirling questions about him being in a city where he has never visited before and how is he occupying his time since he has so much of it. Instead of texting back and forth, involving himself in a discussion that may turn into a phone call from her demanding more specific details, Cidal decides to answer her text later when he is freer to converse in pinpoint dialogue. The last thing he wants to do is to take away intimate time from Wei Mei.

"Who text?" she asks.

"My sponsor. The one who is responsible for my art launching."

"Oh, how nice him."

"That him is a her."

"A woman?"

"Correct."

"She important to have position?"

"She has tons of money."

"That is good. Your art good."

"Oh, no!"

"What?"

"Your portrait is back home. I meant to bring it to New York with me."

"Oh, no worries. I see when I go."

"Back to Rising Falls?"

"Maybe business. Maybe personal."

"The next time I see you I will have it for you."

"Okay."

Twilight kisses the Chinatown sky as they walk out of the restaurant. People and traffic are still everywhere. Their adventure blends in with the night into the call of lateness summons them to return by bus, and then by foot back to the hotel. He escorts her to her room. A hug. A kiss. He goes back to his room. There, he contacts Lady Ila by text, and then she turns right around and calls for a short conversation. He explains how he explored certain parts of the city. Which is partially true. Because in the beginning while Wei Mei was preoccupied with clients, this is what he did. They said their goodnights.

Forty-five minutes to one hour later, there is a knock on the door. Wei Mei steps in after he answers it. Plans are for her to stay with him for the night. Ten minutes into her visit, she gets a call. She answers in Chinese. One minute of talk. She disconnects.

"I will go now." She collects her minimum belongings and heads out the door without an explanation.

33

Maybe there will be some explanation from her the next morning. Or maybe not. This is what Cidal figures. He messages her through WeChat. No reply. He goes down to have breakfast like he did the previous morning. A possibility occurs of a showing of her and her coworkers. Instead of arriving at 8:30, he gets there a little earlier around 7:50, 8:00. He walks into the dining room area nonchalantly. Just like he did yesterday morning. He gets his food and takes a seat in a different spot because the table he sat at yesterday is currently occupied. He starts to eat. Casually, he looks around. The dining room is engaged but not completely full. It's easy to notice that there is no sign of her. He continues eating, checking his phone for messages.

Once he has his fill, after taking his time eating, he rises to leave. When he is half-way across the room, Wei Mei and her friends walk into the dining room. According to the time, it's now 8:35. They make subtle eye contact. Not to avoid one another, but not to make a spectacle over a friendly acquaintance. With the way they glance, each knows and understands this. Her friend, Xia, seems to be aware of this too. The other two, not so much because their unfamiliarity with him.

Cidal goes to his room and sits on the bed. A WeChat message signals. He picks up what Wei Mei sends.

Sorry last night. Will busy today.

He realizes the time aspect of the business she is in. Time ties into money. If he can provide the money, time will march in step. He sends a message back to her.

I will pay to have you for today. I don't want you to miss making money.

There is no immediate response to what he suggests. A waiting period lasts as long as a half-hour or so before she replies.

> *How will you do?*
> *I give you money to spend time with you. You can give some*
>   *to your boss to keep happy.*
> *Okay. I will see.*

About two hours later, a knock on the door. Cidal goes to answer. Housekeeping. He allows the cleaning personnel to do their job while he takes a stroll on the grounds of the hotel.

Wei Mei comes to Cidal's room to see that the housekeepers are doing their job. A cleaning cart on the outside and the door remaining open. She peeks in. No Cidal. So she leaves. Walking down the hall, she stops to send a WeChat message to him. He replies right away. She receives it and goes back to her room. Less than five minutes, Cidal knocks on her door. Without delay, she opens and lets him in. They greet with an embrace; a small kiss. He takes a small envelope out of his pocket and gives it to her. The flap is tucked inside without it being sealed. She whips out some cash.

"I hope this is enough to spend the day with you," he says.

"This is lots," she says. "Why you pay?"

"I don't want your boss to think you're getting out of work. If you give boss some, boss will be happy, right?"

"Maybe. Boss sometime strange. Where you get?"

"From selling my art."

"You good artist to get pay much."

"The one who sponsors me is responsible."

"Oh, yes. I remember. Rich woman. She like?"

"She likes my artwork. What happened last night?"

"Boss no want me to stay. No go without boss tell me."

"Oh, I see."

"Okay, I go now."

"You go where?"

"Go to boss. Tell boss I come back later."

"Okay. I'll wait here."

Wei Mei leaves the room. Cidal sits in a chair waiting for her return. A knock on the door. He holds tight without moving or checking to see who it is, but the person on the other side refuses to be denied. The knocking continues. To see who it is, he goes and uses the peephole. A Chinese woman appears. He thinks it is Wei Mei's coworker and friend, Xia. He opens the door. She is surprised to see him and not her friend in the room. Her English is not very good at all.

"Wei Mei?" she asks.

Cidal understands the language barrier and tries to speak slowly, using hand signals to indicate she will be back. He nods his head and invites her in. She repeats Wei Mei's name. Cidal whips out his phone and uses the translator app to speak to her. After receiving the voice and textual message in Chinese from his phone, she understands. She sits on the side of the bed. The wait is not long before Wei Mei comes back to the room. The two women speak their language while Cidal listens to the uniqueness of the sound of Mandarin. Wei Mei looks at Cidal with a long face. Then, she speaks to him.

"Boss say no." Wei Mei hands him the envelope with the money still inside.

"No? That's not good."

"I have visitors come. Boss want me here."

"Okay then. What time is lunch?"

"Up to boss what time."

"Maybe we can have lunch, got to a park. How long is lunch?"

"Short lunch."

"Maybe you can get extended time."

"Boss say so maybe. I get ready for visitors. Xia get ready to."

"Okay, I'll let you get ready."

"I send WeChat to you later."

"That's fine."

They say their goodbyes. She tells him sorry, and by the expression on her face, she is a bit disappointed by the whole ordeal, but enough faith remains for the possibility of a later encounter.

His room is clean and unoccupied. The staff members are gone. Two minutes after being back, his phone rings. He knows it's not Wei Mei. She only sends messages through WeChat. Instantly he picks up once he sees who is calling.

"Hello," he answers.

"You must be avoiding me, darling." Lady Ila says, sitting outside in the back of her home by the underground swimming pool. She is wearing a summer dress, high-heel sandals, a straw hat, and sunglasses, sipping on a tall glass of ice tea by straw with a lemon around the rim.

"Hey, Lady. No, it's not that. Sorry, I've been a little busy."

"I'm sure you have, but with whom."

Cidal does not say anything.

"Oh, c'mon, darling, relax," she says lightheartedly. "I just want to know how's my artist is doing. Having fun?"

"Yes I am."

"What time does your flight return? You are coming back Sunday evening?"

"Yes. Around 6:35pm."

"Splendid! I will pick you up."

"Okay. Thanks."

"Anything you need to tell me?"

"No. Like what?"

"Oh, anything that's on your mind."

"No, everything's good."

"All right then. I won't hold you. We'll be chatting."

"Okay. Bye."

"Bye."

She disconnects the call and sits in silence.

"You can bet he's seeing somebody," Marsay says, who is also sitting by the pool.

"If he is, why should it concern me?" Lady Ila says. "The poor darling will be very disappointed if he ever crosses me. I have an investment in him. Business and personal. I will do what is in my best interest."

"And I will be at ringside to view the whole show. Please tell when the finale begins. I love fireworks."

Cidal is determined not to take the wait and see approach if Wei Mei will be able to slip away with him for an afternoon delight in the park, so he ventures out on his own. He will not sit idly by in his hotel room and miss the purpose of his New York trip. To visit and to be with Wei Mei. To absorb the sights of experiencing a well-traveled city. All the time he is out exploring, he does not WeChat her once. Every once in a while he checks his phone to make sure he is not missing any messages; however, beyond that there is no second thoughts.

Throughout the rest of the day, he does not hear from her. By early evening, he is back in his room with paper and pencil, sketching out ideas for a new painting. The TV is on low volume. He sits up on the bed, pillow propped up on the headboard, leaning his back against it.

Eventide mellows softly into the night. A WeChat message signals. He does not answer it. He knows who it is. Both he and she realize what will take place without fully knowing all of the details. Moments later, there is a knock on his door. He doesn't even give it a glance. In anticipation of the possible unaccepted arrival, the door is slightly ajar. Wei Mei pushes it open and creeps in, closing the door completely. She walks over to the bed and crawls on top, hands and knees. During these moments, he has never looked up as he continues his sketching. But when she is next to him, he stares at her, drops his sketching board and pencil onto the floor without looking where it lands, he puts his arm around her, and lies peacefully with her.

"Tomorrow morning, tomorrow afternoon, dear, I'm free," she whispers.

"I know you will be," he whispers back.

Not knowing how to answer, without having anything further to say, nothing is said.

34

A giant manmade bird with metal wings touches down. Off the plane and through the terminal, Cidal walks to collect his baggage. A waiting luxury car, part limo is parked with Lady Ila's chauffer standing by. The trunk pops open, the one suitcase and his laptop is placed inside. Cidal climbs into the back seat where Lady Ila is present. She leans over expecting a return kiss after he's been away for a few days. Their lips press. The car rolls off.

"Thanks for the lift," he says to her.

"How was the trip, darling?"

"Adventurous. Never seen New York before. It was nice."

"You couldn't have spent the whole weekend alone in a town like that."

"I wasn't always by myself. But for the most part I was."

She leaves it there and says nothing more. He doesn't want to tilt the small row boat over, so he says nothing to add on to what he said. By route and scenery, he knows this is not the way back to his apartment. The chauffer seems to have gotten word before Cidal arrived to take them to Lady Ila's home. Indeed, this is where they end up, eventually, pulling into her driveway.

"Do you mind staying the night?" she asks.

"No, I don't."

"I know you must be tired and famished from your trip. We can eat and relax. I'll take you back home in the morning. I know you want to get back to your art."

"Yes I do. But I want to be with you too. This is fine."

"Of course it is, darling. I haven't seen you in a few."

"Yes it has been. Well, I'm still the same."

"Are you?"

"I can prove to you that I am."

They go into the house and unload. Slipping into their comforts of having a meal, they share a glass of wine in the sitting room on the same sofa in sparse conversation.

"What are you afraid to tell me?" she asks.

"There is nothing I'm afraid to say," he replies.

"Then why not say it. Because I know you're dying to get it off your chest."

"Okay. When is my next art show at the gallery?"

She laughs heartily. "You are very cute and clever. Very evasive. It all depends on you, lover."

"You mean how much work I can put out?"

"That too."

"What else is there?"

"Who did you spend your time with in New York when you weren't alone?"

"An escort," he says without hesitation.

She is beside herself to hear such candidness coming out of him. "A what?"

"Yes, that's right. An escort who happens to be a friend…I think."

"Amazing!" she says, still in disbelief. "So my competition is an escort."

"What competition? She is who she is. You are who you are. Both of you are unique."

"Thank you for that at least."

"Why?"

"She being an escort means there is no emotional ties she has with you or vice-versa. How long have you known her?"

"I met her before meeting you."

"So before I came into your life, you could afford to pay to be with her."

"No. I was with her one time, and I had to save up to do that."

"Why?"

"Why does any man pay for it? The lack of."

"Oh, I see now. No one else was in your life at the time. No other woman."

"Precisely. And being a man, I have to engage in certain activities to keep things functioning properly."

She throws her head back and laughs again. Once she has the giggles out, she resumes her dignity.

"Now you know," he says.

"Young girl?" she asks.

"Early 30's."

"Uh-huh. So how much money did you spend on her this weekend?"

"Nothing at all."

"So you didn't have sex with her."

"I don't quite remember. My memory comes and goes. When I think I'm in one place, I find out I'm totally in another."

"Ha! You're nothing but a son-of-a-snake. A son-of-a-weasel. You know that's who you are, don't you?"

"Ha ha! If you only knew me, I would get more sympathy. But I'll never ask for it. It's probably better that no one really knows me completely. They would be greatly disappointed."

"This is what I know of you. You're simple but complicated to figure out. I really don't think you know yourself too well. Correct?"

"A simple man with simple needs. That's all I am. I don't ask for the world. And never will."

"This part of you makes you very interesting. Tell me, what is your passion outside of your art?"

Cidal thinks for several seconds. "Without my art, I have nothing. There is nothing that drives me."

"If you could not draw, if you could not create paintings, there is nothing else you would do?"

"I would become nonexistent."

"I have many passions."

"Yes. And it shows. Which one is your greatest?"

"What every woman wants and needs. What every woman greatly desires."

To this, she said a whole lot in just a few words. The lines in-between he reads perfectly. At least he thinks he does. He makes his move for a slow passionate kiss. After the kiss, she tells him:

"It's much more than this. I will never force myself on any man if he does not want me. I will not be crossed up by any man either."

"Why do you say this?"

"Just to let you know the rules of my game."

"I have been, and still am willing to play."

Night smothers the atmosphere. The sunless hours continue until the first crack of daylight, reaching dawn. Through morning rituals of the body accepting alertness out of the slumbering night, to replenishing it with the first meal in order to tackle on the coming of the new day, Lady Ila carries Cidal back to his apartment. A kiss and departure, he sees her on her way. He turns to walk into the building and is surprised that Ms. Pearly is not there to witness his every move.

Everything is where he last left it. Completed portraits leaning against the wall. An unfinished painting on his easel. Nothing has been touched which is quite unusual considering Ms. Pearly has a set of keys to his apartment and is always full of curiosity about how he conducts his life. Nevertheless, she allows him to be who he chooses without much interference. He sets his luggage in his bedroom and comes back to get himself ready to paint without delay.

Sporadically, he takes breaks here and there. A bite to eat if he can find something to munch on. A stroll into the city where there is always enough activity going on. He sits on downtown and throughout town benches to collect his thoughts. Engaging himself in people watching to stir some inspiration for his creativity.

In a sea of humanity, he begins to lose himself. Like a silent shadow his depression encompasses him settling its madness inside. In split moments, he dreams of the ultimate escape from the world around him by transposing into that other existence. The routine of life becomes ever burdensome. Gradually, he feels his passion, for the one and only thing that he lives for, slipping away. No longer is he interested in the creation of everything concrete. His desire for the abstract grows deeper within him. It is in this form his soul rests but he cannot get there. Living in the tangible of the physical provides a roadblock.

In a flutter, he begins to move about. Sometimes sitting, sometimes standing, then walking off the restless rock that weighs heavily inside him, pulling the anchor into a swirling bottomless pit. Everything he has worked up to before now seems like a distant memory. The recent success of his art. Spurred by the connection he has developed with Lady Ila. Intertwining patchwork, stitching together mixed match fabrics of cloths with Wei Mei, unaware of her true emotions toward him. He can be taken or left by her according to the instability of a mild relation. However, these and other outside interferences are never the cause of his depression. A specific event or a simple sadness is beyond what is quickly remedied by action taken against it by curbing lifestyle choices. The battle between mind and spirit is a deadly combination that he cannot escape from or out run. He senses a relapse of his past severe semi-tilted state catching up to him in a 100 yard sprint. The faster he runs, the further the breaking tape at the finish line becomes more in his distant eyesight.

Telepathically, and unbeknownst to Cidal, this sends off a signal to Blue Beans who is wandering around the outskirts of Rising Falls. He is alerted like a high-pitched whistle alerts a dog with the very same effect of driving him nuts. He runs in circles as though his britches have smoke bellowing out of his backside. Then like a 4-alarm fire, he takes off running, aiming his jaunt towards the center of town. His legs oddly moving in a circular pattern as though pedaling a bicycle.

Cidal moves in slow motion while the life of the city remains constant in its usual pace. The desire to keep living is no longer an anthem for his mere existence. It's like the stopper has been pulled and all the liquid content is quickly running down the drain. He feels the other side of himself, that invisible self, taking over his physical nature. Because of these extremities going on within him, he needs a place of solitude. To disappear. To shut himself away from the congestion of everything around him. He decides that home is where he should go. But before he can get out of sight, Blue Beans stands from across the street lurking at him. Unaware of his presence, Cidal walks on absorbing his attention only on himself and not his surroundings.

"I got the call." A voice rings out.

Cidal looks up from where he is walking and sees Blue Beans standing in his path. He stops to avoid walking into him.

"Not today, I'm not in the mood," Cidal says.

"Of course you are," Blue Beans says. "The call came through."

"What are you talking about? What call?"

"The call to join the circus. You do know the circus is coming, don't you?"

"I don't know anything about any circus. I don't read the papers."

Blue Beans laughs his head off almost in an inhuman sound. "You kill me!"

"Don't ask me to do you any favors," Cidal says.

"You'll be doing yourself one once you join the circus. It's a wonderful show. You can't miss it."

Cidal attempts to move around him in order to get by. But Blue Beans slides over to impede his progress.

"Where you're going, sonny? I thought you wanted to join the circus. Your ticket's been punched."

"Look! Cut it out about that circus business! I don't have a clue what you're talking about, so let me be. Maybe some other day when I'm in the right mood I can jostle with you, but not today."

"The circus will find you, my friend. You can't run from it. You can't escape it. It is where you are. It's always around."

"And what's your role in all of this?"

"I'm the ringleader."

"I ain't a bit surprised. You fit the role perfectly. Deuces. I'm out."

This time Cidal is successful in walking around him. Blue Beans does not make an effort to stand in his way. With his signature half-crazed grin, his uneven eyes follow Cidal walking pass him and down the street.

Maybe he needs to paint, to create to get himself back on track. He sits there staring at the portrait he has already started, and still nothing is of the utmost importance to him. He used to get inspiration through his work. The only reason why he exists is to do what he loves regardless of income or material gathering. Now, the painting cannot stir the slightest emotion in him. It is as drab as dispersed dirt. His spirit is not attached to his own creation. It is alien to him. Sick of it, sick of life, sick of himself, he goes to his room and collapses onto the bed, hoping beyond imagination that everything could disappear and he along with it.

35

Lady Ila and her good friend, Marsay, take an early evening stroll through the park to enjoy the pleasant weather while walking two cocker spaniels on leashes. Both dogs belong to Marsay. Lady Ila helps out by walking one of them.

"He actually told you what was up on his trip to New York?" Marsay asks in almost disbelief. "He didn't deny it at all?"

"I really didn't know what I was expecting," Lady Ila says. "She must be my competition."

"No, Ila. A prostitute? This is your competition? I'm not buying it."

"An escort is what she's called by his definition."

"What's the difference?"

"One is paying for sex. The other is paying for companionship. This is what I'm told."

"Oh, yeah, right! It boils down to the same thing, girl. It's just a fancy term they substitute it for to make it appear like something it isn't, but it really is."

"Marsay, I'm not stupid. I know exactly what time it is. But the thing that gets me is he didn't admit to having sex with her. He says he didn't quite remember what transpired."

"Oh, come off of it! He expects you to believe him? Shame on him for even trying. He knows you have better sense than that. At least I should hope so. What are you going to do with him now?"

"I will not play paddy-cake with him. I'm beyond foolish games. And he knows that. I made my point extremely clear. He's not going have me burning on one end of the candle and she on the other."

"Yes, this is true. Having you one weekend, and he goes to be with her on the very next weekend."

"With one phone call, I can alter his current situation when it comes to his art prospects."

"Do you think he's a good artist? Maybe he can make it on his own now."

"All art is subjective. It's not how good or terrible an artist is. It's the exposure of their work that makes them who they are. Nothing else. I've given him just a little exposure to test the waters. I can do much more if he plays by my rules. But it appears that he's disregarding them."

"No less with a prostitute."

"No. I don't think she's just a prostitute. There's maybe an emotional connection. No matter what it is, I have given him the resources through royalties and exhibitions of his art for him to turn around and hand it to a hooker to spend the whole entire weekend with. If this is how he's crossing me, he's going to have to deal with me on another level. I'm too mature to be made a fool of."

"What's your plan?"

"My plan is nothing. He will devise his own. I will not play the role of desperation. He has to come through me. If anything happens, he will have to initiate it. If he doesn't, his artistic fate lies in his own hands."

"Will you give him the benefit of the doubt?"

"Again, this is up to him. If there is doubt, there can be no benefit. If there is no doubt, he will continue to reap the benefits of all I have done for him. Artistically and intimately. I share no man if I can help it."

"No woman can help her man from being shared. Regardless of how good of a woman she is. Men are going to do what they do. Period."

"That may be so. But if I am aware of it, that's a different story. I refuse to deal with it. Especially, when I'm holding all of the resource cards."

"He may play you."

Lady Ila laughs. "I encourage him to do so. He will only be playing himself. Playing himself to back to where he started before I made my entrance into his life."

"After all that you have done for him, what if he refuses to continue as your lover? Where will that put you?"

She processes her thoughts before she answers. "The older I get, the more I'm totally convinced that there are no absolute answers to anything. I haven't the slightest idea. However, your question should be, where will that put him?"

Days go by, four or five, but less than a week. There is no sighting of Cidal entering or leaving his apartment. Ms. Pearly is sure to keep a watchful eye out. His door has a *Do Not Disturb* sign hanging on the doorknob. At different times she plants an ear to the door to find out if she can hear anything. Silence. She understands he is his own bizarre self and that an occurrence like this is not unusual. Temptation rises for her wanting to knock and call out to see if he would answer, but she quickly decides against it.

'I don't know what he could be doing, if he's even in there,' she says to herself. 'You never know about that rascal.'

Blue Beans caravans the streets, singing an odd song he's made up, laughing and talking to himself. He grabs the attention of those he passes. The onlookers are not fazed by his antics. They slow their pace to observe, and then quickly move on. It does not matter to Blue Beans, because trying to impress them is the furthest thing from his mind. His only purpose is to be a nemesis to the only one he calls out to. He goes on making a spectacle of himself, reveling in the fact that he knows something that no one else knows. This carries him up and down the streets not having a care in the world.

Back in New York, Wei Mei's baggage is packed and setting on the bed of her hotel room. Her face is solemn. She refuses to give into any emotion of the current situation she finds herself in. Her friend, Xia, stands nearby. They speak the language familiar to both of them. There are no long extended plans when it comes to their business. They move by need and circumstance. By the seat of their pants. Short-term decisions are made quicker than a sneeze. Most often not by them, but through the authority that runs the business. It has been decided that it is time to journey onward onto other pastures. Not unfamiliar territory. Not another city within the US. Not even going north of the border into Canada. They have toured the North American continent for more than ten months. A split decision made by the boss they learned a few hours prior. Back to China. Through Beijing and back home to Shanghai.

Wei Mei sends out a WeChat message explaining to Cidal in a few words, a short choppy sentence of her unforeseen change of schedule. She is not expecting an immediate response. His reply will come at a time when there is nothing to say, nothing else to do to alter what has already been set in motion. Besides, how can he prevent fate? How can he stop the wind? Whatever unsure plans they had for each other is now very certain. Nothing will happen…unless?

More days go by. Still there is no sight or sound. Everything in Rising Falls goes on as usual. People transport themselves through vehicle or by foot; they seem to care not only about their own well-being, but in their eyes, there is empathy for those they pass. Each one seems to live by the notion: *someone else's shoes can fit your feet.*

Ms. Pearly constantly observes the door of Cidal's apartment during the whole time of his solitude. The sign still hangs on his doorknob of not wanting to be bothered. In her mind, she feels that she has to intervene to make sure everything is fine with him. He should never be upset because of the concern his landlady has for him. She knocks and glues her ear to the door. Nothing. She knocks again and calls out.

"Hey! You in there? You okay?"

There is no response. She waits. More than a minute goes by before she knocks again.

"I'm just checking to see if you doing okay," she calls out again.

Her curiosity is too great. She takes out a set of keys and proceeds to unlock the door to discover that the lock has been changed. The key fits inside the keyhole, but unable to turn. She withdraws it and tries again with the same results. She checks other keys on the chain. She is certain that the one she has is the correct one. However, she tries two other keys that are similar. Again nothing.

"You think you're slick, don't you? You making sure no one bothers you. But I have every right to. I'll be back. Don't you worry about that!" She leaves.

Less than an hour later, she returns but her results are no different than before. She feels action is required which may go beyond her legality. She walks away and whips out of her mobile phone to make a call.

Within 15 minutes, a police patrol car pulls into the parking lot of the apartment. Ms. Pearly is sitting outside in a lawn chair waiting for their arrival. Two African-American officers get out of the vehicle and casually walk towards her. She rises to meet them.

"We're looking for a Ms. Pearly," one officer says. "We received a call…"

"That's me," she interrupts, knowing how the procedure goes and didn't want to belittle the time. "Follow me."

As they enter into the apartment building and up the stairs, Ms. Pearly explains to them what has taken place the last several days, which is nothing, and her role in trying to find out if there is something to discover outside of the norm. They reach Cidal's apartment. One officer pounds on the door with the side of his fist.

"Mr. Sewell! Rising Falls Police Department! Let us in!"

A few more attempts to get a response, but to no avail. The officers took the precaution in taking matters into their own hands. With much effort, they barrage in, nearly tearing the door off of its hinges. Before entering, they advise Ms. Pearly.

"Ma'am, you better stay back until we search the premises. We'll call out if we need you."

The officers glance around the apartment as soon as they step in to discover nothing is totally out of place. A painting on an easel. Portraits lined neatly against the wall. A window is open. Without their knowledge, on the outside of the window, Blue Beans barely holds onto the ledge by his fingers. It is obvious he has been inside of the apartment for some unknown reason. Even in this dire situation, everything seems to be a joke to him. That half-cocked smirk is constantly a permanent fixture on his face. His body slightly swings, dangling two floors up from the ground. The cops never drift over towards the window. Their precision of police procedures carries their search from kitchen to the other parts of the small apartment, being very cautious at every turn, every step. They call out Cidal's name again, identifying themselves as law enforcers. The door to the bedroom is slightly ajar. With care, they push it open.

Ms. Pearly remains on the outside of the apartment in the hall. She is anxious to find out what is going on by sticking her head inside the doorway slowly exploring the room.

One officer calls out to her, "Ma'am? Could you come here please?"

As Ms. Pearly enters the apartment, Blue Beans could not continue his hold any longer and releases his fingers. Falling two floors down, he collapses onto the ground with a loud thump. This quickly gets Ms. Pearly's attention. She shoots a sharp eye towards the open window, but quickly ignores it. She rushes into the bedroom to join the officers.

The very first thing that she sees is writing on the wall in big bold print.

ERASE ME FROM YOUR MIND AND FROM YOUR HEART. FOR I CARE NOT TO BE REMEMBERED.

Blue Beans is clearly way down the street, walking his crazy walk, swing his arms along the way. He does not appear to be affected by the fall from the window. He stops and laughs insanely out loud in a silly, eerie way. Then he says in a quiet tone.

'Ha ha. My friend has finally joined the circus. This is not farewell. It's only welcome. Glad that you're able to join us.' He goes into that same laughter and continues down the street singing, 'I helped him join the circus! I helped him join the circus!'

A row boat drifts upon a great body of water. Heading further and further away from the shore. Cidal lies in it. Eyes closed. Very still. Not a single move of a muscle. Throughout the atmosphere, his voice sounds out in a cool, relaxed demeanor:

Not raveling in the mist of discontent
Nor muddling in the sorrows of self-pity

Neither do I masquerade to save face for melancholy dis-
    grace
Never would I allow life's trials to get the best of me
In each road, there is a bend
All I want to do is to ascend

Disenchanted with the whim of life's abundant despair
Bickering fools who haven't a clue
The burden for unenlightened buffoons I no longer want
    to bear

The best of life is what's in it
I lived it through and through
Now, I no longer want to partake in it
Because I did what I had to do

In everyone's existence, it comes a time when enough is
    enough
The calculated remnant of reality is a bluff
No longer will I try to decide what's good is good
or what's rough is rough
The hour has come for my anticipated departure to be
    abrupt

To sever myself from the ties of foolish worldly games
Not even caring if anybody knows my name
I do not fantasize to linger on to age-old wonders
Right here!
Right now!
Boastfully as I long to put my body and soul asunder

There are those who seem to believe that a short life is a
    waste
And that longevity is wisdom based
Popular for one to eagerly face
The desire to reach for elderly grace

Popularity equals stupidity
For I choose not to carry on and to wade
in my own iniquity

Trying not to offend, simply to comprehend
Reasons to defend, why I need to ascend!

Let me ascend!
Because I see the end so clearly
For my soul have grown restless and weary
At last I am at the end of my rope
To wallow not in languish hope

Let me ascend!
The beauty and ugliness of this world is for you
to take or for you to give
For I no longer care to live

Let me ascend!
Death on earth actually starts at birth

With a Higher spirit's permission
I look forward to my next challenging mission
Because my time here was only a brief intermission

So let me ascend!

While I take my last breath
And before my life ends
This last message I send

Live not for yourself, but for others

Remember me never
Goodbye
And forever

As the row boat continues its drift into the middle of nowhere, ahead in the short distance standing upon the water, there flows in the wind a feminine garment of lavish lavender. Without emotion, Mother Goddess awaits the arrival of her son.